Rosey in the Present Tense

Rosey in the Present Tense

Louise Hawes

Walker and Company

New York

First published in the United States of America in 1999 by
Walker Publishing Company, Inc.;
first paperback edition published in 2000.

Published simultaneously in Canada by Fitzhenry and Whiteside,
Markham, Ontario L3R 4T8

Lyrics on page 11 are from "Unchained Melody."
Lyrics by Hy Zaret. Music by Alex North. © 1995 (Renewed)
FRANK MUSIC CORP. All Rights Reserved.

Library of Congress Cataloging-in-Publication Data
Hawes, Louise.
Rosey in the present tense / Louise Hawes.
p. cm.
Summary: Unable to accept the sudden death of his
Japanese-American girlfriend, Rosey, seventeen-year-old
Franklin finds that she has come back to him as a spirit and
eventually realizes that he must let her go.
ISBN 0-8027-8685-5
[1. Death—Fiction. 2. Grief—Fiction. 3. Ghosts—Fiction.
4. Japanese Americans—Fiction.] I. Title.
PZ7.H3126Ro 1999
[Fic]—dc21 98-8857
CIP
AC
ISBN 0-8027-7603-5 (paperback)

BOOK DESIGN BY JENNIFER ANN DADDIO

Printed in the United States of America

2 4 6 8 10 9 7 5 3 1

For Butch, at last.

Hana no negai
hanano no tsuyu to
naru mi kana

—TEMBO, 1823

Acknowledgments

Deepest thanks to Marc Jacobson, my designated First Reader; to Robin Jacobson, who cried *before* the last page; to Marcia Amsterdam, who heard this book's voice; and to Emily Easton, who edited it with her heart as well as her eyes.

Rosey in the Present Tense

Rosey spreads her arms out like an airplane, then dive-bombs off the rock. She does it the way a little kid would, without fear, without looking down. Her bones feel small and perfect as a bird's when she lands in my arms. She laughs, throwing her head back and showing me her white teeth, her throat. I love you, Rosey Mishimi, I think. But I don't say it out loud.

"Now where, Intrepid Leader?" she asks when I set her down. She shades her eyes with one hand, staring past me into the tangle of creepers and low-hanging branches. Behind my sunglasses, I could be looking along the trail the way she is; she probably thinks I am. Actually, I'm watching Rosey, studying her, like I'm going to be tested, like I don't want to forget anything.

She's wearing jean shorts, rolled at the bottom, and a sleeveless T-shirt with the Heart Burn tour logo faded into secret writing. She's pushed her hair behind both ears, something she does a lot, even though it always falls back over her face a few minutes later.

"I don't know." She sighs this big exaggerated sigh. "You promise a girl a tremendous waterfall, then you get us lost in the deep, dark woods." She steps closer to me, her eyes opening like hidden pockets. "Franklin T. Sanders, did you do this on purpose?"

She's looking up at me, and I remember the first time I saw her last September, how I stood there, numb, dumb, and staring. It's not like she's the only Asian girl who's ever gone to our school or anything. It's just that she was so full of contradictions—soft and strong, quiet and loud, all at the same time. She moved down the row of lockers like a dancer, yelling something smart and fast at her friends, shielded eyes peering from under that curtain of hair. I couldn't stop looking at her, and she was onto me right away. Even while she wrestled with her combination lock, even while she joked with the tall girl next to her, she was watching me watching her watching me.

Eight months later, I'm still watching. Still nuts for what I see. "I'm sure there's water around here," I tell Rosey. "I can smell it." I tense up, like some kind of dog on a scent. And it's true. The air is heavy, ripe as wet leaves. "If we find it, you're going to be totally and absolutely blown away." I move in close, put my hands around her waist. The tips of my fingers nearly meet. "And if we don't," I add, getting within kissing distance, "we could do worse than deep, dark woods."

I'm all puckered up when I hear it, the sound of small feet in dry grass. I stand still, listening, waiting until I'm sure. Then I grab Rosey's hand and run right into the tangle. I round one corner, charge down the small snaky trail, and there it is. It's not a big falls, compared to Victoria or Niagara, I guess. But I see again how it hits you coming out of the shade and the woods. It starts at the top of a table of rocks and spills down two or three levels into a tiny pool. Because it's the only spot where no trees are growing, it's smack in the middle of a shaft of sunlight, and there's a permanent rainbow hanging in the air above the water.

I can hear Rosey catch her breath. She puts one arm around me and stands next to me. I don't say anything, I don't need to. Still, I feel like the two of us are talking somehow, like I'm finding this place all over again. I look at the water, spilling over itself, listen to it chatter, and I feel dizzy in a good, overflowing kind of way.

Rosey closes her eyes like she's dizzy, too, then opens them again. "In Japan," she tells me softly, "my grandparents had a saying." She watches the shiver, the dance in the air. "I think it's a quote from a Zen monk, and I may not have it perfectly, but . . ." She moves to look directly into my eyes and says seriously, slowly, "Goodness! Gracious! Great balls of fire!"

It takes me a second before I see the shifty glint in her narrow eyes, the smile. "I think you've got your Zen and your Jerry Lee Lewis mixed up," I tell her. Fifties and sixties rock and roll is one of Rosey's passions—she's probably the only person under ninety on the planet who owns a turntable, and we spend half our time at her house hopping up and down to change those old records.

She doesn't answer me. She's looking at the water again, her arm tightening around me. "God, Lin," she says, for real now. "Who would believe something like this in New Jersey? It kind of stops your heart, doesn't it?"

I know what she means. About the waterfall and about New Jersey. My mom and I moved here eight years ago, after Dad and she got divorced. I remember thinking that a place with so many highways and factories and supermalls had some nerve nicknaming itself the Garden State. But there's actually green around here if you look for it. Once a friend and I walked out the back of a department store. We crossed the parking lot, and ended up by this old empty barn, knee-deep in heather. New Jersey heather!

Rosey and I take turns now, jumping into the cramped pool and trying to find the bottom. The water is frothy, bubbling against the rocks like a Jacuzzi. After, covered with goose bumps, we find a dip in the rock table, a warm cubby, where we can unpack the food. It took some hard climbing and scrambling to get here, and it seems no one else is up to it. We have the place to ourselves all afternoon, reclining like Roman degenerates at a banquet, popping grapes and cheese squares and cinnamon doughnut holes into each other's mouths.

When it's time to go, I don't want to. Rosey is stretched out beside me, one leg wrapped carelessly over mine. She looks almost transparent in the sun, fragile and strong at once—those contradictions again. I don't know why, but that long white leg makes my eyes fill up, makes me want to protect her, watch over her, even though she's really independent and doesn't much need it, I guess. "In Japan," Rosey announces now, "my great-great-grandparents had a saying. It's very old, and I'm not sure I remember it right."

"I know, I know," I interrupt her, grinning. "Doo wap ditty, she bop she bop."

She grins back. "No," she says, "not exactly." Then she pulls my face down to hers, easily, gracefully as if she were lowering a window shade. She kisses me, and it's the same as always. My insides turn liquid, and I feel as though parts of me are being sucked out, running away. "I think I love you," she says.

We really should leave. The sun is already too low in the net of oak branches behind us. It's going to be hard to see the trail marks on the path we took here. But I roll over, one arm under my head, one arm around Rosey, and watch the violet-colored sky. It's the first time Rosey has said she loves me. It's the first time any female, except my mother, has said it. No fireworks go off, though. It doesn't feel tingly or exciting or new. It just feels right. So right I don't need to say it back. I pull her close, like I want to make sure she's not going anywhere, then stare up at the sky and breathe out, long and slow.

1

Leonard Stiller had an annoying habit of leaning forward whenever Franklin spoke. As if he thought his seventeen-year-old patient was about to tell him the meaning of life, or at least who was going to win the pennant. It had been a lot easier, Franklin realized, to put his thoughts down in the journal than to hold a conversation with this man.

"So," Dr. Stiller said, shifting in his chair, holding up the small brown loose-leaf. "You don't see anything remarkable, anything askew, in what you've written here?"

"Askew?" Franklin turned on the leather couch, caught Stiller's eyes glancing off him.

"Unusual," the psychiatrist explained, placing the notebook in his lap, balancing it across his scarecrow knees. "Different."

Franklin nodded, then thought. Rosey is unusual, he decided. Rosey is different. But he knew Stiller didn't mean that.

He studied the man's placid face, the deep, empty eyes that gave out no light. "I give up," he said.

Dr. Stiller smiled, uncrossed his legs, and leaned forward again, his perfectly trimmed beard and gray-flecked brows swimming toward Franklin through the afternoon gloom. "Haven't you noticed," he asked, "what you've done here?" Now the notebook swam forward, too, falling open a little, the corners of its white pages gleaming. "Hasn't it occurred to you, Franklin, that all these memories are written in the present tense?"

"Oh, that." Franklin felt a familiar shame, a niggling failure to measure up. "My family's always on me about that." He turned around, settled back in the couch. "My friends, too."

"It's been over six months since Rosellen's death, Franklin." The older man's voice wasn't scolding or judgmental; it washed over Franklin, a slow, sad rain. "Six months since the accident, and yet you're still talking about her as if she's alive."

Franklin struggled to keep the film from starting, the reel that played in his head anytime someone mentioned the crash. *Talk*, he thought to himself, as Rosey's bright pink jeep rounded a curve. *Talk, for God's sake.*

"You asked me to put down everything I remember," he told Stiller. He felt the tears just behind his words, pushing, jostling each other like a concert crowd. "That's the way I remember it." For nearly two months he'd been jotting them down, bright pieces of the past that came alive as soon as he started writing.

"I see." Stiller leaned closer. "What do you think about that, Franklin?"

It was the same sort of question the doctor had been asking

him for weeks on end. "How do you feel about that, Franklin?" when the antidepressants made him dizzy. "Would you like to interject something here?" when the school counselor attended a session, shaking her head, using words like *despondent, clinical, withdrawn.*

"What do I think?" repeated Franklin, weary and angry at once. "I think I'm sick to death of thinking." And I'm sick of coming here, he wanted to add. Of taking my pills like a good boy. Of trying to help everyone else forget.

"I wonder what would happen," Stiller said, the notebook back in his lap, the tips of his pale fingers pressed together, "if you rewrote those incidents in the past tense."

Franklin stared at the arched fingers of his therapist. A childhood game glided like a large, lazy fish into his mind. *Here is the church,* he thought, *here is the steeple. Open the door, and see all the people.* Then Rosey's car turned down the road toward Sundaes Unlimited, and he closed his eyes.

"Do you think you could do that for me, Franklin?"

"What?"

"Do you think you could take this journal back and choose one of the entries to rewrite?" Franklin opened his eyes, the peak of hands collapsed, and Stiller sat up. "Describe things in the past tense? Put these memories behind you?"

Rosey behind me, Franklin thought. *Rosey in front of me, Rosey beside me.* Lidded eyes, dark hair with copper highlights flashing like waves. *Ring around the Rosey, a pocketful of posies . . .*

"Franklin?"

Ashes, ashes, we all fall down.

"Did you hear me, Franklin?" Stiller asked. "Do you think

you could do that for me?" He stood up, held the notebook across the distance between them.

Franklin rose and nodded again. He took the book back, and when Stiller reached out with his other hand, Franklin shook it, then hurried out of the office and downstairs into what was left of the afternoon.

"How did it go?" His mother's voice had the same cheerful, tinny sound it did when she asked him about tests at school. But she looked tired, the skin around her eyes and mouth looser, paler than he remembered. When had that happened?

"Okay, I guess." He shed his nylon parka, headed for the refrigerator, avoiding her eyes, her worry.

Ever since he was little, Franklin had been painfully aware that what happened to him happened to his mother, too. He had always had to stay cheerful, healthy, because if he didn't, they both paid. "It's a gene, that's all," he remembered Rosey saying. "A mother gene, and there's nothing you can do about it."

"Dud called," his mother told him. He felt her watching him now, memorizing his moves. "He said everyone's going to the Blue Lantern tonight."

"It's Friday, Mom." He emerged from the fridge with a bag of pumpernickel, a jar of mustard, and the last of a roll of salami. "They go to the Blue Lantern every Friday."

David Dudden had been Franklin's best friend through junior high and three years of high school. For almost that long, he'd been a karaoke freak, dragging Franklin and anyone else willing to tag along to the local k-bar on under-twenty-one night. Sweating in the spotlight, supremely happy, and gyrating obscenely, Dud treated them to off-key renditions of top-forty hits and, when the DJ could find them, songs by a band that everyone else had forgotten. "Red Dwarf is coming back," Dud always told his astonished audience. "You'll see. One day they'll be on top again."

Deftly, automatically, his mother slipped a wooden chopping board onto the counter before Franklin had time to cut into the salami. "You haven't gone out with the gang in a long time. It might be fun."

He shook his head, turned around to look at her. "Mom," he asked, "when you were in high school, did you call the group of kids you hung out with 'the gang'?"

She smiled crookedly, like a kindergartner. "No," she admitted.

"Have you ever heard me refer to Dud and Company as 'the gang'?"

Again the apologetic grin. "No."

"In fact," he added, spreading the meager slices of meat wide so there would be enough to cover the bread, "did you ever hear anyone except kids on bad sitcoms call their friends 'the gang'?"

Defeated and much more cheerful, she brushed his hair back from one ear, then reached above him to the cupboard for a plate. "Nope."

"I rest my case." He closed the sandwich, put it on the plate, and patted its top with a flourish. He walked past her, carrying his late lunch toward his bedroom. "And yes," he told her over his shoulder, "maybe I'll go. Okay?"

He didn't. They both knew he wouldn't. But it bought

time, time when he didn't have to see his own grief reflected in her face. Time he could spend in his room, silent and suspended like some slow beast in hibernation. He lay on his bed, Rosey's photo looking at him from the nightstand, their favorite Righteous Brothers disc on the CD player, louder and louder until he didn't need to think.

Lonely rivers flow to the sea, to the sea. The lyrics swelled, trickling like syrup through the music. *To the empty arms of the sea.* Now he couldn't help hearing the words, couldn't fight the wave that rushed him. *Lonely rivers cry, wait for me, wait for me.*

I'll be coming home, wait for me. Under the music, outside his door, he heard a timid, scratching sound. "Go away, Mingo," he yelled at the door. "Bad cat!" Rosey had loved his Siamese, loved the way Mingo rode on people's shoulders, his cream-colored body draped like a fur, the way he licked your face, his raspy tongue wetting your nose and cheeks. Since the accident, though, Franklin had hated the sight of his pet. The cat was sixteen years old, the same age Rosey had been. But that made Mingo close to ninety if you counted in cat years. What was wrong with God, anyway? Why did a spoiled feline who refused to eat anything but the most expensive cat food in the store (the label showed a long-haired Persian on a pink satin cushion) deserve to live longer than his girl, his own Rose?

It wasn't fair, it wasn't right. In fact it disproved the entire existence of God—even if you'd been dragged to church every Sunday for years and still had a Bible with your name in gold letters on the cover. God couldn't exist, Franklin decided, because no God, whether he had ten arms with a flaming sword in each, whether he'd given his only son to the world to be hung on a cross, or whether he was formless and past understanding—no God anywhere could help loving Rosey. Could kill her just like that. In an instant. For no reason. No damn reason at all.

He knew what they'd say, his friends, his family, all the well-intentioned people who kept waiting for him to "get over it." They'd say it was unhealthy to shut himself up like this, that Rosey would want him to get on with his life. They'd say he was only making it harder each time he pictured her sitting beside him, her small head nestled against his chest. He was living in a fantasy world, they'd say, if he kept hearing her laugh, like bubbles caught in her throat. Take your medicine, they'd say, see your shrink, they'd say. And all the time, all along, what they really meant was, forget.

But how could he? Why should he? When remembering Rosey was the only relief he felt; when closing his eyes and pretending she was touching him was the only way to stop the constant, lonely rattle inside him. So he did it now. He lay back and let her come to him, let her breath fall like sunlight against his arm when she leaned down and asked again, "So why can't we do it, Lin?"

She tickled his eyelids with the tips of her hair. "It's not like we're going to live forever. We could be dead tomorrow, and never know what great sex is like."

He remembered laughing, pushing her away. "A," he told her, "we're immortal, and B, if my mom comes back early, the sex will definitely not be great."

They had joked about being the world's oldest virgins. It seemed that every time they'd come close to finally "doing it"—their clothes in awkward folds under and around them, Franklin's blood racing to all his extremities, even ones he wouldn't need—something had stopped them. Either the police decided to patrol Harrington Field for the first time in recorded memory, or, like that last time, Franklin hadn't wanted to risk being caught by his mother.

Of course, he knew that his mom knew he had the same urges everyone else did. (He remembered the time she'd started to complain, shortly after his fourteenth birthday, about the way the bathroom tissues kept disappearing, how she'd stopped herself suddenly, turned, and walked, embarrassed, out of his room.) And, if you'd pinned him to the wall, he would even have acknowledged that his mother had probably, at some fuzzy point in the distant past, felt those urges too. But since the divorce, it was a topic they never discussed. He'd even avoided showing too much physical affection for Rosey in front of her. As if his arm around his girl meant one less hug for the other important woman in his life. It wasn't true, it was silly. But somehow, he'd always been careful.

Now, when he wished with every muscle and sinew he'd been a lot less careful, he remembered Rosey's eyes closed, her breath coming hard and fast, and her whole body pressed against his. "Oh, God, Rosey," he said out loud, turning over on the bed, wrestling the sheets into uncomfortable ridges. "You were right." He thought about dying like Rosey had, a virgin. He wondered if that wasn't the only fair thing to do. It didn't seem so much to ask, since he couldn't bear the thought of touching anyone else, much less having sex. *Forgive me.* He said it inside his head now. *Please forgive me, Rose.*

"For what?" Rosey asked him. Her voice sounded real,

solid. He put his hands over his eyes, trying to imagine the face that went with it, trying to make her stay.

"It wasn't your fault," she said. "I'm the one who didn't wear a seat belt. I'm the one who didn't see that truck. Who . . ." Her voice trailed off, dwindled to a sigh. A sigh that came, not from inside Franklin's head but distinctly, clearly, from just beyond his left ear. "Did you hear me, Lin? Open your eyes. I need you to look at me."

But he didn't. Instead he increased the pressure of his palms, blocking out as much light as he could. He didn't want to lose her, he didn't want to open his eyes and find the room empty. "Rose." He groaned it more than he spoke it, balling his hands into fists now, savaging his eyes with his knuckles. "Rose."

"It hurts if you don't see me, Lin." She sounded so sad, so alone, he unclenched his fists, stopped thinking about himself. "I can't feel my arms or legs when you look away. I need you to see me, Lin-san."

Franklin took his hands from his face; then, opening his eyes and blinking, he saw her, actually *saw* her. Rosey Mishimi was sitting beside him on the bed the way she always had, the way he knew, by all the rules of logic, she shouldn't be, couldn't be—would never be again.

2

Rosey was wearing the same jeans and UCLA T-shirt she'd worn the day of the crash. But there were no rips or holes in them, no dirt stains or blood. As there must have been. As there had to be. Franklin watched her cross her long pony legs, stare around his room. "It's like coming home, after you've been away," she said. "Everything seems so small." She looked back at him now, her eyes sheeted, glass. "Even you, Linny."

He couldn't speak. He couldn't move. He couldn't break the spell. *If this is what happens with Stiller's happy pills,* he thought, *I'll pop them forever; I'll take them every day for the rest of my life.*

"I'd forgotten the colors. There are no colors where I was." She touched his cheek, but he felt nothing, nothing more than a breeze, the mildest bit of wind on a summer day. "I didn't miss them, though. Not until I heard you crying."

"Crying? Who was crying?" he asked, the tears still wet on his face. "Real men don't cry."

"Oops. Must have been my other boyfriend," she told him, smiling, tracing his nose, his lips with her weightless hand.

"Don't go." It wasn't what he should have told her, what he would wish later he'd said. But Franklin felt dizzy, nauseated, and underneath, sharper than the nausea, worse than the dizziness, was the fear. There was something wrong, something off about the way the light shifted when she moved, about her feather-soft touch. "I'll do anything you want," he announced, still frozen. "I'll kill myself, I'll take more pills, anything. Only please, Rose . . ." He felt the muscles of his jaw tighten. "Please, don't disappear."

"I won't," she told him. "I can't. I don't know how to get back." She took her hand away, stood up, and walked, a strange trail of light, a sort of shadow in reverse, following her to the window. She looked out at the afternoon, the leafless oak branches that were already budding, that would fill out to shade the whole house by summer. "I didn't feel anything, Lin. Not my hands or my feet." She shook her head. "Nothing for the longest time."

He couldn't bear her turning away, couldn't stand not seeing her face. He scrambled from the bed, stood beside her. "It's okay, Rose," he whispered, as if he were soothing a child. "It's going to be okay."

She faced him now. "It's just hard to get used to, that's all. I didn't want to come back, you know. Not until I heard you."

"You're here now, that's what counts," he said. He studied the clean T-shirt, the spotless jeans. "It doesn't hurt anymore, does it?"

She shook her head, wrapped her arms around herself. "It feels good," she told him, "to see you again." She grinned, her head to one side, appraising. "Uncut hair and all."

He smiled, wanted to laugh out loud. To jump for joy. "I haven't cared much about the way I look lately," he admitted. When had he last glanced in a mirror? Or changed his underwear? Even brushed his teeth? "But I'll go skinhead if you say so."

Her eyes, the charcoal eyes he'd imagined, remembered, cherished until they burned his brain, studied him. "You look puffy, Lin-san. Like you've been crying forever."

He remembered the weeks he couldn't get out of bed, the months of moving underwater, going through the motions. He remembered the pink pills, the red pills, the conferences at school, at Dr. Stiller's. And even though every second of that time was clear in his memory, the ache of missing her as fresh as an open wound, he couldn't tell her. He only nodded.

"Have I been gone long?" Her arms still folded, she gazed at him matter-of-factly.

"Since August," Franklin told her. "Since . . ." He hadn't dared touch her yet. Something had held him back, some nameless dread that everything would end if he tried. But he did now. He reached out to unwrap her arms, cup her face in his hands. She slipped away, shattered like a strip of sunlight when he stepped into her. He felt the warmth, smelled her vanilla sweetness, but touched only empty air.

"Rose!" Panicked, he stepped back, and she reassembled, filled up space again. "Rose, there was a funeral. Did you . . . ? I mean, were you there?"

If she'd forgotten, he hadn't. There were images, sounds

that kept revisiting him in ugly flashbacks, bits of old reality that had the staying power of dreams: the shock of the recorded organ music in the small chapel; the way Mrs. Mishimi's tears had mixed with her mascara, pulling it in shaggy tracks down her round, white face; the glistening handles of the casket disappearing under shovelfuls of dirt and pieces of still-green clover.

"Funeral?" She moved to his desk, sat on the chair, like anyone, any flesh-and-blood, living, breathing human being. She closed her eyes, concentrated. "No, Lin-lin. I wasn't there. I was . . ."

"Last August," he repeated. "After the accident."

"August?"

"Six months ago, Rose." He hated the vague, lost look when she opened her eyes, wanted to wipe it away. "But it doesn't matter, Rosey. None of it matters. We can be together now."

"Time is so hard to get used to again." She said it blankly, mechanically. "It stopped when I . . . you know.".

Again, he had no words. Again, he nodded.

"It didn't seem like dying. What happened, I mean. I was bigger, Lin. Much bigger." She stopped, considered. "Or smaller. I was asleep. Or awake.—It's so hard to explain." She gripped one arm of the chair, focusing on nothing he could see. "It was like a veil, Linny. Like the thin skin under an eggshell. I was that close to thinking and feeling, you know?" She turned, saw him at last. "But I didn't want to."

"You've come home." He said it too quickly, felt his breath catch, as if he'd been running uphill. "You've come home at last."

She stared at him, a thirsty, deep look, before she stood up. She grinned then and walked to him, tried to take his arm. "As home as I can get, I guess," she said, leaning her head against his shoulder, seeming not to notice that where she touched him, her hands scattered into particles, dancing bits of light.

"And you'll stay, right?" He looked down on the thick dark hair with its pale part, the narrow shoulders. It was strange how short the months he'd spent with her seemed now, how long the time without her. He wanted to lock this moment, to keep it forever like a wing trapped in amber. "Right, Rose?"

"Maybe." She tilted her face up to his, smiling wider. "Provided you get better taste in music." She pointed to the CD player, and he realized the Righteous Brothers album was over and the next disc had slipped into place. It was a new group Dud had recommended.

"Heavy metal," he explained apologetically.

"That's not heavy metal," Rosey told him, sounding almost like her old self. "That's deadweight."

He laughed, but he didn't trust this miracle. He followed Rosey around the room, his rapture tempered by the horrible suspicion that it was all too good to be true, that he was making her up. That any second he could lose her by some misstep, some failure to stay alert. So he watched her, kept the shape of this new joy always in front of him as they talked.

Which is why he didn't turn around, didn't take his eyes off her face, when his mother knocked on the door and came in. While Rosey was alive, Helen Sanders had usually waited for an invitation before opening the door to her son's room.

But lately she'd taken to walking right in after a token tap or two.

"Mom." When Franklin finally turned to look at her, he was too happy to bark about his privacy. "Isn't it great? Isn't it beyond great?"

"It's great to see you smiling, mister," his mother conceded. "To what do we owe this minor miracle?"

Rosey stood up. "Hello, Mrs. Sanders. I know it's late." She smiled conspiratorially at Franklin. "We had a lot of catching up to do."

Franklin's mother didn't answer, didn't let Rosey finish speaking before she rushed ahead. "The last time I saw a smile like that," she told Franklin, without even glancing at his girl, "was when you and Rose got those tickets to the Fifties Fest in Bloomfield."

Franklin remembered the velveteen skirt Rosey had worn to the show, the saddle shoes she'd bought at a thrift shop. "You looked so hot that night," he told her, then added, grinning, "Of course, you still sang off-key!"

His mother's mouth tightened suddenly, pulled into a small, stricken O. "I'm sorry, love." She reached out to touch him but pulled her hand away, let it flutter to her throat. "I didn't mean to bring back anything painful, . . . I . . . I just . . ."

"Hey," he told her, "that's okay." He leaped off the bed now, grabbing his mother's waist and sweeping her around the room in a galumphing, sloppy two-step. "In fact, everything's going to be terrific from now on," he chortled, whirling faster and faster. "Because this is no minor miracle here. This is Rosey!" He brought them to a sudden halt in front of his girl. "In the flesh and crazy as ever!"

"What are you talking about?" His mother, breathless from following him, laughed nervously. So did Rosey.

"Rosey, of course," he told her, panting, waving his arm toward the bed, the double laughter washing over him. "Rosey's come back."

He saw Rosey's frightened smile, watched his dance partner stop and aim her fiercest, saddest mother-look at him. But still he didn't understand. "Tell her, Rosey. Tell her you're not leaving anymore."

"Franklin." Now both his mother and Rosey were shaking their heads. "Franklin." His mother sat on the bed gingerly, slowly as an old woman. "Oh, my poor baby."

A butterfly-shaped blush had spread across Rosey's nose and cheeks, a sure sign she was going to cry. "She can't see me, Lin." She waved a hand in front of Mrs. Sanders's face. "Can't hear me, either."

"You mean . . . ?" Franklin saw the nervous way his mother had taken hold of her own elbows, cradling herself. The old urge to protect her, spare her, bubbled up in him.

Fighting tears, Rosey made a sound halfway between a sigh and a sob. "I mean, I'm not really here. I'm nowhere." Collapsing onto the bed beside his mother, she lowered her head into her hands, letting the tears come. "Oh, Lin," she wailed, her voice shrill as a lost child's, "I'm nothing but a ghost!"

May 10, Rosey's birthday

Harold Mishimi is a short man, at least two inches shorter than I am. Still, there's something about him, something kind of impressive, like a small tree with a thick trunk. Not that he's heavy, either, just solid, with a deep voice that belongs to the boss in a gangster film, not an Asian-American accountant with bifocals.

"Come on in before the mosquitoes do," he says to me, shutting the screen door as soon as I'm inside the kitchen. "Want some OJ?" He holds up a fresh glass.

"No, thanks," I tell him. "Is Rosey around?" I always ask this, even though I know she's waiting for me because I just talked to her on the phone.

"Sure," Mr. Mishimi says. "Go on back." Rosey's family lives in a rambler all on one floor, so I just have to walk through the kitchen and take a right, and I'm knocking on Rosey's bedroom door. Usually I love the smells in the hall, partly her grandmother's cooking, partly incense. But today there's another, sharper odor. I'm wrinkling my nose when Rosey opens the door.

"It's the paint," she tells me. "Wait till you see."

"I already do," I say. There's a neon pink streak on the front of her favorite T-shirt; it's covering the right side of James Brown's face, but she doesn't seem to care. The half-moons of her finger-nails are lined with pink too, and there's a big dot of paint on the tip of her nose. "What happened?" I ask. "Were you attacked by a gang of ripe watermelons?"

"Very funny," she says. "Where's my present?" She looks like a little kid in those overalls, one shoulder strap already fallen around her waist. Every time I see her, I can't believe anyone can be so skinny and so sexy at the same time. "You said we could use it right away."

"We can. As long as you haven't painted your car doors shut." I wave the box I'm carrying in front of her, so she'll know I didn't forget. Then I turn toward the garage. "Let's go."

I lead the way back down the hall, but Rosey ducks in front of me. "Wait! Wait!" she commands as we reach the door at the end. She puts her hand on the doorknob, then takes a deep breath. "Da-da-da-DUM!" she announces. "Presenting the latest innovation from Mishimi Motors. The car that looks good enough to eat—" She opens the door, and the smell of fresh paint is overwhelming. "The Bubble Gum Machine!"

It's a neat old jeep, the real thing. I can still see some army camouflage where she hasn't finished painting, and the gearbox is covered with a thick rubber skin, like a black glove. "This is outra-geous!" I say it real hearty and loud, the way my father used to sound. A birthday ribbon is still tied to the T-bar, and the tires look brand-new. "Completely outrageous!"

Rosey's already in the driver's seat. "Want a ride, soldier?" she asks, winking. I throw my box onto the jeep's floor, then hop up beside her, being careful not to touch the shiny paint on the outside of the door. I don't close the window flap; the smell is getting stronger.

"I can't really take it on the road till Dad gets the plates. But we can cruise the driveway." Rosey scuttles out of her seat, then presses a button on the wall. She's in again and backing out the jeep before the automatic doors have even opened.

"Rrrrummmmm! Rrrrummm!" she says for emphasis. "Hear this baby purr?"

The asphalt is cooking in the hot sun, tiny stars winking on and off across its surface. The air is close and muggy, but the smell of the Bubble Gum Machine is not as strong out here. "An automotive triumph," I tell her, grinning. Rosey throws the jeep into park and lets the engine idle. I wave my hand through the open flap. "And built-in AC, too!"

I notice the box by my feet. "Here," I say, handing it to her. "You don't need to wait for plates to use this."

She's a kid again, tearing open the cardboard flaps. I wish I'd remembered to use fancy paper, but she doesn't seem to notice. It's the most expensive birthday present I've ever bought anyone, but I didn't spend any time at all picking it out. I knew exactly what to get.

"Oh, my God, Lin!" She pulls it out of the box and holds it up. "A portable CD player!" She throws her arms around me, still clutching the player, nearly womping me in the head with it. "I can't believe it. It's too perfect!"

It is. We sit in the driveway for over an hour. Rosey sets a beach umbrella up over the Bubble Gum Machine and brings out half her

CD collection. Every time one of us recognizes a song and starts singing along with it, we switch discs.

"It's an old story," Rosey howls, her head back, the words moving like beads up and down her throat. "But it's new to me."

Just when it's too hot to stand, Baba, Rosie's grandmother, appears in the driveway with two glasses of grape punch.

"My baby's gone, gone, gone. Whoaoooooooo."

I sing along with Rosey, nodding to Baba, taking the misty glasses off the tray she's holding. Rosey presses the pause button, slips the CD out of the player, and puts it in the discard pile with the rest.

Baba is a tiny woman, always smiling, the only one in the family with an accent. It's so thick that sometimes I can't understand what she's saying, but today she adds pantomime. "Too hot," she says, wiping her brow. "Hot enuf fly eggs."

Rosey bursts out laughing. "Fry eggs! Where'd you hear that, Grandma?"

Baba pauses, confused. The empty tray slaps against her thigh. "Mailman say. Is not okay?"

"It's okay," I tell her. "It's perfect."

Unconvinced, Rosey's grandmother shakes her head. "Maybe not perfect, I think," she says. "But at least, I attempt." She points at Rosey. "This one, she forget Japanese words I tell to her. Cannot say back simple children's rhymes."

In the sticky shade of the umbrella, Rosey's eyes widen. "Hey, Grandma! That's not fair. I've got that hashi poem nailed. You know, the one about the bridge over the lily pond?"

"Hmmmm." Baba nods. "Yes, you say poem more perfect than my English." Suddenly, she's not smiling, but I see the same devilish look in her eyes Rosey specializes in. "More perfect if poem about chopsticks over pond."

"Chopsticks!" Rosey sits up straight. "Hashi doesn't mean chopsticks. It means bridge."

"It mean chopsticks, way you say." Baba's smile is back, broad, triumphant. There are two dimples, like a child's at the corners of her mouth. "Got to put music in word. Got to make end of word go up high for bridge. Ha — shi. Way you say, no one make it over pond. Everybody drown." She shakes her head, still smiling, then turns toward the house.

"Hashi. Hashi." Rosey's concentrating, hunched over the steering wheel. "Hashi." Her voice doesn't rise on the last syllable the way Baba's did. It drops every time, and finally she gives up, grins at me. "Guess I'm all wet, huh?" She leans back, waiting for me to make my next selection.

I paw through the discs in the bag, then put one into the player. I slip my sunglasses out of my shirt pocket so I can watch Rosey without her knowing. "Bet this'll stump you," I tell her, smiling fiendishly, settling into my seat. Actually, I hope she guesses the cut on this album right away. I can't wait to see her belting out her Janis Joplin imitation, her eyes closed tight, every note missing by just a bit. I stare at her when she starts singing, her throat straining against the words, and I wonder if I'd love her half as much if she learned to carry a tune.

3

Franklin didn't like lying to his mother. But it was clear he couldn't tell her about Rosey. Not without winning a lifetime membership in Stiller's loose bolts club. "Mom," he said, mustering an adult, sober tone. "I didn't mean to upset you just now."

Helen Sanders looked at him, encouraged.

"It's just that sometimes Rosey seems so real to me." He tried to remember the terms his therapist had used over and over, until Franklin had stopped listening. "I guess you could say I'm going through denial." He glanced at Rosey, hunched, shoulders still heaving. "Dr. Stiller says that's all part of the process."

Rosey sniffed. "Great," she said, her voice threatening more tears. "Now I'm a figment of your imagination."

"It's not that I'm crazy or imagining things," Franklin announced, caught between them, trying to make both feel better at once.

Rosey wasn't placated, and his mother shook her head for what seemed like the thousandth time. "No, honey, I'm sure you're not," she said, her fond, sad voice suggesting that yes, she was afraid for his sanity. "It's just that you've been spending too much time in here by yourself." She sighed and turned her attention to his room, as if the tattered movie posters, the pyramid of empty pizza boxes, the SLIPPERY WHEN WET sign he and Dud had smuggled off Loftus Bridge, were somehow to blame for everything.

"Dr. Stiller says a familiar environment speeds healing." He thought that was what he'd heard. He followed his mother's gaze around the room, then sat on the bed, treating himself to the warmth, the shine of Rosey beside him. "I'm okay, Mom. Really, I am."

"I've been putting in too much overtime lately," his mother said, taking a new tack. "I'm hardly home at all."

"That's not it." Franklin corrected himself. "I mean, nothing's it. I mean, nothing's wrong."

Helen Sanders ignored him. "It's the Overton account. No, it's Fletcher T. Overton. He keeps changing his mind." She paused, shook her head again, the small gold shapes dangling from her ears shaking too. "So-*called* mind, that is. I should just tell Mr. That's-Not-Quite-It to take his vanities and his custom kitchens and put them—"

"Mom." Franklin certainly didn't want his mother to take time off from work. For one thing, she loved writing TV commercials, even if it was only for cable. And for another, the last thing he needed was more heart-to-hearts like this one.

"You've been great. So has Dr. Stiller. And I feel fine. Really fine."

"Honest Cowboy?" His mother had resurrected a game they used to play when he was little. She poked an imaginary gun into his ribs.

It was Franklin's turn to shake his head, sigh. Slowly, he reached for the sky. "Honest Cowboy," he said. He felt ridiculous enacting the ritual in front of his girl, but if it made them both happy, he didn't care.

It did. As the finger-gun was removed and his mother smiled hopefully, Rosey brightened, sniffed again. "Hey, sharpshooter," she asked, "can I play, too?" A familiar, sly grin, a grin that filled him up, warmed him, spread across her features. Now she too leaned forward, stabbed a finger into his side. It broke into splinters of light when it touched him, but he pretended to take offense.

"Hey, watch it," he warned, laughing. "You're looking for trouble."

"I am not," his mother told him. "I'm just trying to understand." Her eyes were the same shade of blue as his, pale with lots of gray in it. "To give you someplace to live beside the past."

"Don't worry, Mom," Franklin said, feeling only slightly guilty. "I'm right here, and I know the difference between yesterday and today." He needed her to think he was on the mend, not having dialogues with thin air. He needed to wean himself from Stiller, the watching, recording, monitoring. "I know what's real and what's not."

"Then why—?"

"It's like all the things Rosey said and did are still here, even if she's not." He glanced at his girl. "You know, all those lousy jokes? Those made-up ancestors?"

"Lousy jokes?" Another sniff. "Whose jokes are you calling lousy?"

"So you're saying you've realized there are parts of Rosey you can't lose?" His mother's voice had gotten lighter, younger.

"Sure."

"Only those parts don't exactly work the way they used to," Rosey added, determined to sulk. She kissed him on the cheek. "Admit it," she said. "You didn't feel a thing."

"I did," Franklin insisted, lying. Then he saw his mother's surprised look. "I mean, I did . . . some hard thinking, thanks to Dr. Stiller. Mom, he's been a big help."

His mother's eyes slid from the gray to the blue side of the scale, and her smile was dazzling.

Seizing the advantage, he added, "In fact, I feel so much better, I don't think I'll need to go back." When it came down to it, the only part of seeing Stiller he'd enjoyed was keeping the journal. And now he didn't need to.

"We'll see," she said, in a way that made him suspect he wasn't free of those hateful visits yet. "I guess you've decided to skip dinner again," she added. "I've got a plate in the oven for you if you want it later."

Franklin *was* hungry, hungrier than he could remember being. He glanced through the window blinds, noticed it was already dark outside. How long had he been lying here, listening to music, feeling sorry for himself? Lately he lost track of time a lot. "Thanks," he said. "I think I'll pass." He didn't want to waste a minute, didn't want to spend one second away from his lost-and-found girl. "I'll eat a big breakfast to-morrow."

After his mother had closed the door, a resigned half-smile on her face, he lay back in bed, begged Rosey to nestle the way she used to in his arms, their legs twisted around each other. It wasn't the same, there was no pressure, no sweet weight on his chest. But it didn't matter. Because there was her scent, her warmth, the husky voice he could listen to forever. Even if she was telling him she didn't belong here. "I don't fit, Lin-lin. You can see I don't. There's someplace else I'm meant to be."

"You do too fit," he assured her, proving it by folding himself tighter, closer around her. "There's no place else, Rose. No one who needs you like I do." He let Mingo, who had slipped through the door as his mother left, settle beside them, kneading the back of Franklin's sweater with his claws.

"One time in Tokyo," Rosey said from under Franklin's chin, "my great-great-grandfather didn't speak for three days. When my great-great-grandmother urged him to communicate, he finally said, 'Old fish don't swim as fast as young ones.'"

The cat rolled over now, exposing his white belly, begging Franklin to scratch the soft place, tight as a drum skin, under his ribs. Franklin loved Rosey's made-up relatives. He reached one lazy, generous hand toward the Siamese, watching his girl. "Okay, I'll bite," he told her, smiling. "What's that mean?"

She curled up to look at him, a strand of hair fallen across her eyes. "I haven't got a clue, but I feel like an old fish, so I thought I'd mention it."

Franklin studied her slim fingers, wanted to kiss their tips, one by one. "Old fish don't look half as delicious as you do," he said.

"I'm sorry, Lin-lin." Rosey pulled her hands away, as if she'd read his mind, and stared at him mournfully. "I know I should just be glad to see you again. And I am, but suddenly I feel like I've been dragged up onshore and don't know how to breathe. I feel old and tired. I want to rest."

It scared him, shocked him, to think she wasn't as happy as he was right now. How could she be gasping for air, when he was inhaling huge, glorious drafts of relief? "We can rest, Rose. We can rest together." Hunger still tightened his gut, but he unfolded the maroon-and-green quilt from the bottom of his bed, let it fall over them both.

"I'm not *sleepy* tired, Lin. I'm just tired." She twisted in his arms, but the quilt didn't move, only the air shimmered, shifted a bit. "In fact, I don't think I can sleep. I don't think ghosts do."

"You're not a ghost."

"What am I, then? Figments don't sleep, either."

"You're not a ghost, and you're not a figment." He nuzzled her dark head, remembering how it used to feel, precise and unalterable, solid underneath him. "You're Rosey Mishimi. The one and only."

"And you're pretty beat, mister." She must have seen the yawn he'd tried to turn into a grin. "Why don't you sleep, and we'll figure all this out in the morning."

His eyes snapped wide. "No!" He felt like someone with a terminal illness, someone who might not wake up if he went to sleep. "I'm not tired. I want to be with you."

She smiled then, her old I-love-you-even-though-you're-a-dork smile. And they gossiped about school, about who was going out with who since Rosey's accident. They talked about how he'd done on the SATs (not well; he'd taken them in a drugged haze without caring), about college (he'd told his mother he'd go to State, though he hadn't thought about it once since he'd promised). Each time he felt his eyelids get heavy, Franklin forced himself awake, found some question to which he desperately needed the answer. "What was it like?" he asked now, brave in her arms. "You know, after the crash?"

She sat up, let him rest his head in her lap. He felt only the pillow, but it was warm, as if it had lain for hours in the sun. Later, he would wonder why books always described ghosts as cold, when Rosey was so full of heat and light. "At first," she told him, "I didn't know what had happened. When everything went black, I thought a storm was coming. I knew I should leave, but I just lay still. I tried to get myself moving, told myself I had things to do. I concentrated on all the reasons I should get up—my family, my job, my okay-looking boyfriend."

Franklin looked properly outraged, but stayed where he was, snug and settled as a kitten. "You mean your adorable, hunk-macho-studly hero?"

"Yeah, him." Rosey's voice softened, purred. "Anyway, I finally forced myself to walk around, check out the car. And you know what?"

"What?"

"It didn't look bad. I mean, I thought I could probably start it up. But then I found this girl lying in the middle of the road. She was covered with blood."

He closed his eyes again, not wanting to see.

"I didn't realize it was me. Pretty silly, huh?"

His Rose, alone. Facing it all alone. Franklin shuddered, opened his eyes.

"I thought I should stay with her until help came, but it kept getting darker and darker. So I started walking instead, moving toward what looked like a sunrise, a break in all that black."

"Rose?" Franklin searched the face he'd wished for, held in his mind and heart all these months. "Where were you? Where did you go?"

"It was nothing I can describe. Not a place, I mean. It was more like a feeling." She shook her head, tried again. "I was so thankful, so glad—it was as if gratitude were gravity, holding everything together. And everyone. There were others, Lin-san. I didn't see them, not exactly. Didn't even talk to them. Not in words. But I knew them; they were all so precious to me."

"Precious," repeated Franklin, nuzzling. "You're precious to me."

"I don't know how long I was with them. It seemed forever, but then I heard you crying. The others heard it before I did, Lin." She shook her head again. "Long before. I guess I was so new, so happy there, you couldn't reach me. But suddenly, straight through forever, I knew it was you."

Franklin swallowed, remembering. "I missed you so much, Rose. It hurt to wake up. It hurt to go to sleep."

"That's why I'm here, Lin. That's why I left them, why I found this memory"—she glanced at her fingers, wiggled them—"this half-body. All I had to do was follow your voice. Back the way I'd come," she told him. "Back into the dark."

"Back to me." Overwhelmed with his own joy, his own gratitude, Franklin heard only her words, not the regret that chimed like a tiny warning bell behind them. "Back to you and me."

4

When the first stripes of light forced their way through the slats of his window blinds and angled across the bed, Franklin panicked. "Rose?" He sat up, rifled through the sheets as if she might have gotten tangled up in them. "Rosey?" He called louder now, more frantic. He was furious with himself for letting go, for falling asleep. "Rosey!"

"I watched you while you were sleeping," she told him, stepping into a streak of sunlight that crossed the wall and carpet. She nearly washed away then, the light rushing to meet her, bleaching out her chin, her shoulders. "You looked a lot cuter than you sounded."

He laughed with relief, bounded out of bed, and hugged her around the waist, his arms shivering her into bits of light, closing on nothing, his nostrils reveling in the familiar Rosey smell. "You mean, I snored?"

"I'm not sure I'd call it snoring," Rosey said, walking out

of the circle of his arms, becoming herself again. She sat now on the foot of the bed. "It was more like earth moving or demolition or something."

He laughed again, thankful to have her back. To still have her back.

"What on earth is that cat up to?" Curious and suddenly unromantic, Rosey was watching Mingo.

"Oops. Guess I fell asleep without letting him out," he said. "He just needs a quick trip to the litter box." Franklin headed for the door, but Mingo beat him there, his back arched like a Halloween cartoon, his short fur electrified. Complaining loudly, the cat threw its body against the door as if it were trying to break it down.

Outside in the hall he heard a low whine, a shuffling sound. As he opened the door, a black, shaggy paw forced its way through the crack, then without acknowledging Franklin or Mingo, a pudgy cocker spaniel clawed its way into the room, leaped onto the bed, and began growling at Rosey.

Still outside the room, David Dudden watched his pet through the doorway. "That dog is nuts," he observed calmly. "First, he wouldn't stop chewing my dad's wallet; now he's got a sheet fetish."

"No, he doesn't," Franklin said. Dud could be trusted, he knew. "Thornton's just glad to see Rosey."

"What?"

Franklin stood up, crossed the room. "You'd better come in." He closed the door behind his friend. "Sit down, Dud. This may take a while."

Dud tended to look surprised even when he wasn't. There was something about his gaunt, barely there body, his huge eyes and dark brows, that gave him the appearance of a startled waif. Now, at the mention of Rosey's name, his eyes widened further and he glanced uncertainly, warily, at his dog.

Thornton was still preoccupied with Rosey, alternating yaps and growls, long ears stiff with alarm. She was trying to settle him, giving him pats he couldn't feel, talking soothingly. "It's me, boy," she said. "Remember? Rosey of the doughnut crumbs?"

It helped a little. Thornton's growls turned to low rumbles, as if he were talking under his breath. "See?" Franklin told his friend. "Rosey is here. Right in this room."

Dud seemed more confused than elated, and it wasn't hard to figure out why. Every Saturday, for the last half year, he had come to see Franklin. And every Saturday he had been greeted by the same morose figure, the same groggy, pathetic character who'd told him he didn't want to hang out, didn't want to go anywhere, maybe next week. But here, tall and grinning, was the friend he'd been missing. The friend who'd lost his girl and was now apparently completely crazy. Instead of sitting down as he'd been invited, Dud backed toward the door. "Look, Lin," he began. "I know how rough this has been for you. I know—"

"He thinks you're nuts, Lin." Rosey sighed, looked at Franklin, heavy-lidded, reproachful. "Maybe you are."

If this was nuts, he'd rather be around the bend than back where he'd come from. If it was crazy to love waking up again, to feel the planet spinning under his feet and know it was carrying him someplace wonderful, who cared? "Okay, okay," he said. "This isn't easy to take in all at once." He turned to his friend. "Dudster, please. Sit down? Is that a lot to ask?"

Dud moved to the bed, studied his dog. Thornton seemed calmer now, his chunky, clipped tail the only part of him that moved—a nervous twitch, a wag cut short. Slowly, as if he didn't want to give up the option of standing again and making a run for it, Dud sat down beside his pet.

"Not there!" Franklin winced as Dud and Rosey overlapped and his girl splintered, dissolved into shivering motes. "Rosey's sitting there."

They both stood up at the same time, Rosey reassembling, Dud groaning. "God! Get a grip, Lin." Dud leaned down to stroke Thornton, then looked at his friend again. "Listen," he said more softly, eyes angry and sorry at once. "This has got to stop. They're going to be putting you in a very tight jacket if you keep this stuff up."

Franklin knew he was right. He'd known all along, but he'd hoped things would be different with Dud. Hoped he'd have someone to share this fullness, this joy, with.

"Those sleeves that tie in the back?" Dud added, trying to lighten things. "Trust me. It's a fashion statement you don't need to make."

Franklin nodded. It didn't matter. Even if Dud thought he was a lunatic, he would draw the line here. For himself. For Rosey. "I don't care what you think, Dud. She's here. She's real."

"Real?" Rosey seemed to think he was trying to convince her as much as Dud. She gave him a grateful, misty smile. "I wish."

"Don't say that!" Franklin hated her doubt, her sad smile.

"I'm sorry." Dud looked apologetic. "But someone has to snap you out of this." He slapped his thigh, and Thornton bounded off the bed, stood panting at his heels. "What do you say we get you out of here. I need to replace Loretta's fuel pump. How about a trip to the junkyard?"

"I don't know." Some part of Franklin didn't want to put Rosey to the test, wasn't ready to expose her to the real world. He had to admit, though, it would be like old times, the three of them in Dud's ancient Plymouth Fury, Rosey's ebony hair fanned out behind her when they finally got up some speed. "Maybe later." He gave Rosey a cautious, sidelong glance.

"It might be fun," she said, looking so hopeful it made his chest pull tight.

Because there was nothing she could ask for he wouldn't try, because this was such a simple thing, Franklin nodded. "Okay," he told Dud. "Rosey's vote swings it, two to one. She wants to go."

"Christ, Lin. Don't do this." Dud's tone was midway between pleading and threatening. "She's gone. Rosey's gone." He turned toward the door, his dog following him. "And I'm here." He gave Franklin the lost-orphan look that was his specialty. "I've *been* here. But honest, Lin, I'm not sure how much more of this I can take."

"You think I'm a basket case, don't you?" Franklin stared at his friend, then at Rosey, who watched him from the bed. "You think I'm insane."

"I think I wish I'd loved someone as much as you loved Rosey." Dud stared solemnly at the tips of the designer sneakers he'd run into treadless nubs, and Franklin knew it was true. Homely, girl-crazy Dud was tired of being a cliché, of making clever, jaded comments while his friends walked off with the beautiful women who never even looked at him.

"I spent an entire year running to Bresler's Salvage replacing Loretta's rusted innards." Dud's voice was quiet, confessional. "You spent that year with Rosey."

So shut up. Franklin knew that's what Dud meant. Even Dud. *Shut up and be glad for what you had. Stop rubbing it in my face. Take your pills and forget. Please, for my sake, just forget.*

Dud shrugged now, making amends. "You want to converse with air? Be my guest." He opened the door, and Franklin followed, waiting until Rosey had slipped out between them. "Just don't expect me to make room for your ghost in the front seat."

"No problem," Rosey told them, her pale shadow turning bright as fire when they stepped outside. "I'll ride in the back."

Dud's Plymouth reminded Franklin of the model car he'd left in his shorts pocket when he was seven. After his mother put it through the wash cycle, it had emerged paintless and battered, a demolition derby survivor.

But Dud, who lavished constant attention and weekly waxes on his old heap, seemed oblivious to the car's shortcomings. "Come on," he said, wrestling into first and maneuvering the Plymouth into the junkyard's parking lot. "Let's get Loretta back in mint condition." He leaned across Franklin to force open the handleless passenger door.

Franklin climbed out, patted the car's lusterless front fender, eaten away by a sprawling rust spot shaped like a glove with six fingers. "Loretta hasn't seen mint condition since the seventies." He said it cheerfully, without malice, opening the rear door, grinning at Rosey.

"All present and accounted for?" Dud frowned, as his friend held the door wide, then stepped back as if someone had really gotten out to join them. Shaking his head, he turned and walked toward a squat, corrugated building that looked as if it had been assembled from the sides of old railway cars.

Franklin tried not to notice how the fierce sun bouncing off the tin walls turned Rosey's skin paler than ever, so pale he had to squint to find her beside him.

A bear-shaped man in green coveralls was talking on the phone when they walked inside. He waved noncommittally, then turned his back on them to finish his conversation. Dud wandered the rows of junk, exploring, and so did Rosey. Here, in the musty, oil-smelling dark, she gained dimension again, seemed distinct and real.

Gratefully, Franklin watched her pick her way around piles of used tires, one-of-a-kind hubcaps, bumpers, and grilles. As if she were searching for something in particular, his girl ignored the shelves of auto supplies and recycled refuse that Dud browsed and walked instead to the back of the room. She stopped just inside the big open door that looked out across the junkyard.

Franklin followed and stood behind her, gazing at the mound of twisted cars and trucks that reached all the way to the horizon, the jagged silhouettes of useless antennae and upended tires pointing at the sky. He surprised himself as he studied the wrecks—some of them late models, still bright and reflecting the sun, others a lot older, old enough to have turned brown or orange or the deep red of damp clay. They looked beautiful, he thought, tossed all together like that.

Yesterday he wouldn't have been able to stand there, quietly contemplating a field of smashed cars. Not without dissolving into tears. But yesterday he didn't have his Rose back. There were two of them facing the heap of torn roofs and pleated hoods. Two of them, and that made all the difference.

"Think this is right for Loretta?" Dud came up behind them, stepping right through Rosey to survey the tangle of wrecks. "There was an auto freshener shaped like Marilyn Monroe, but I liked this better." He held up a tiny figurine. "It's a dashboard Elvis."

Franklin endured Rosey's splintering, her momentary dissolution, held his breath as the light from the yard swallowed her, then spit her out, whole again. Now she stood on his other side, considering Dud's find.

"Only if he still gyrates," she decided, laughing.

Laughing. She used to do it all the time, Franklin remembered. Anything would trigger her, would send her into paroxysms, bubble chambers where she howled and cried until you couldn't help laughing right along with her.

"Do his hips move?" he asked. He could have kissed Dud, even the tiny slick-haired Elvis, for putting that smile on her face.

"They used to," Dud said, pushing the figure's plastic torso with his thumb. "But he's a little rusty."

Rosey shook her head, still giggling. So did Franklin.

"Help ya?" Off the phone, the man in overalls came toward them. He had a jowly face, thick arms.

"Hi." Dud reached for the man's hand. "Remember me? I got mag wheel covers here?"

"No." Bear Man stared at Dud's hand without shaking it. "But you musta got the last pair, 'cause there's none left."

"Actually," Dud said, "I don't need covers this time. I'm looking for a fuel pump. For a Plymouth." He pointed to the door they'd come in. "That one in the lot."

The man didn't turn around, just continued staring at Dud. "Only got Chevys and a Toyota right now." He shuffled back toward his desk. "Oh, and a Taurus. Just came in today."

"Guess I'll have to go the dealer route." Dud looked discouraged, as if he were already handing over his money.

"Suit yourself." The man was halfway to his desk when Franklin saw it.

"What's this?" he asked. He took the small machine off the shelf beside him.

Bear Man turned. "What d'ya mean, what is it?" He looked irritated, and his phone was ringing again. "It's a CD player, that's what it is."

"I know." Franklin looked at the player. The brand, the finish, even the scratches, were familiar. "I mean, where'd you get it?"

"Offa jeep." The man stopped, remembering. "The one that girl got killed in last summer." He looked at them briefly over his shoulder, then ambled to his desk to pick up the phone. "Bresler's Salvage," he said. "No, nothin' yet. Try me on Thursday."

He hung up, turned back to them. "Yeah, up on Forty-nine. It was in all the papers." He shook his head and wiped one massive paw on the greasy left leg of his coveralls. "They say she landed clean across the highway. But there's hardly a dent on that jeep, parts good as new."

"Oh, jeez." Dud sucked in his breath, a whistle in reverse. He touched Franklin's arm. "Hey, I'm sorry."

"Yep. Thrown more 'n thirty feet," Bear Man volunteered. "Little thing, I guess." Then he noticed their faces. "Didn't know her, did ya?"

Franklin stared at his lovely girl, the girl no one else could see. He concentrated on her skin, her velvet eyes, blanked out the image of her body tossed through the air like a rag doll.

Dud put an arm around his friend. "We just came in for a fuel pump. We'll try someplace else." He backed Franklin away from the CD player, as if he didn't trust it to stay on the shelf, as if it might follow them outside. "Thanks anyway."

Franklin was quiet as Dud nosed the Plymouth out of the lot. He sat, his head and shoulders swiveled, staring at the backseat. Dud peered into his rearview mirror, satisfied himself the car was empty, then broke the silence. "I'm really sorry, Lin," he said again. "I guess this expedition was a pretty dumb idea."

"There it is!" Rosey stood up, bracing herself against Franklin's seat, pointing to a spot across the junkyard. "See?" Franklin looked where she was pointing and found it too.

It signaled to them like a neon flag from the middle of the sea of wrecks. Perched at a rakish angle, its tireless front fender planted on the trunk of another car, Rosey's pink jeep looked out of place among the fractured, weathered hulks around it. Jaunty, whole, it winked in the sun, and its persistent bright- ness made Franklin close his eyes. Made him open them quickly and turn to check that she was still there, his pale Rose, whose hair was just as he'd remembered it, fanned out in slender streamers behind her. And who stared with longing at her old car as they pulled away.

Date of Memory:

June 22, the last day of school!

Sissy Wells can't sit still. She's passing notes and dropping things, giggling and waving good-bye to everyone in sight. Sissy's leaving with her family for a trip to Barbados today. Her father's packed her stuff in the car, so all she has to do is hop in after eighth period and ride to the airport.

Not that it's much easier for anyone else. The last day of classes is always rough. Even for the teachers. Mrs. Rogers is about as itchy as I've ever seen her, laughing at Hughey Fine's lousy jokes, looking at the clock every other minute. Guess she's got vacation plans too.

Rosey is Mrs. Roger's pet, so she's spent half this period in front of the class—first, she gave out the cupcakes with pink sprinkles Mrs. Rogers made for everyone; then she handed back all the papers Mrs. R. forgot to give us during the year; now she's helping judge this dumb math contest that's supposed to make us all feel like winners. With my luck I'll come in last, and Rose will give me that sweet, it's-okay-with-me-that-you're-a-total-moron smile.

I don't care, though. It's finally summer. And Mom said we could bring Rosey to the lake with us in August. We've gone every year since I was a kid, even before the divorce. But this year will be the best of all. Rosey's in front of the class now, helping Mrs. R. explain integers or something. But all I can think about is lying beside her on the dock, our skins wet and sweaty, her voice like a low secret.

I start thinking about the ways the lake will change. Rosey won't laugh at my prayer to Neptune the way Mom or Dud always does— she'll probably add some special ritual or sacrifice—and who knows, maybe we'll actually catch something besides sunnies this year. And Mom will finally have someone to take with her when she prowls those antique stores on the way into town. And at night, as our campfire turns into whispers and sparks, as I breathe in the remains of the day—smoke and sweat and the last hot dog no one could eat—I'll be holding Rosey next to me.

I'm so busy thinking about this summer that the final bell of the final day catches me off guard. It sounds like a fire engine or an ambulance is running right through my blood. I didn't hear who won the contest; I don't even know why Mrs. R. has tears in her eyes. I suppose it has something to do with the giant card she's holding—did anyone ask me to sign it? I can't remember.

Dazed, I stand up, and it's over. People are rushing by me, thumping me on the shoulder, rushing out the door. I'm the last one to leave. I stumble out of the room like a sleepwalker.

Dud and Rose are talking with Amy Chester and Charlie Strand in the hall. "So, should we celebrate our freedom with pepperoni?" Dud is crazy about pizza, and he celebrates just about everything with pepperoni. But Rosey shakes her head.

"Can't make it, Dud-san," she says. "It's my grandmother's

birthday." She looks at me. "You go if you want, Lin. Maybe you can stop by later."

"No way." I shake my head too. "I'm not missing Baba's party." I don't know too many old people, but if they're all like Rosey's grandma, I wish I did. She doesn't speak great English, and I sure don't speak Japanese. But she and I sort of understand each other. Mr. and Mrs. Mishimi are nice, but they always look a little shocked to see me walk in their house. Baba isn't surprised at all; she knows just why I'm there, and she's happy for Rosey and me.

So I tell Dud I'm sorry. "Okay, buddy? Pizza's forever, but Baba hasn't got that many birthdays left."

"How old is she?" Amy asks. I like Amy, even though she spends so much time with a jerk like Charlie.

"She's ninety-four if you're Japanese," Rose explains, "ninety-three if you count American-style."

"Huh?" Amy glances at Charlie, who's paying no attention at all; he's turned his back to us and is giving a victory sign to someone down at the end of the hall.

"In Japan they figure you should get credit for the year you spent in the womb. So over there, you're a year old when you're born, two on your first birthday. Got it?"

Suddenly, Charlie's all ears. He turns to Rosey, his smile full of teeth and the plastic braces he's been wearing forever. "Hey, that's great," he says. "That means you can drink in bars a year before the rest of us, right?"

Rosey rolls her eyes, loops her arm through mine. "See you, Chuck," she says. "Don't let Dud O.D. on garlic, okay?"

It's warm outside, a moist day with the sort of pale, stringy clouds overhead that mean suffocation, not rain. I take my shirt off and walk in my T-shirt. Rosey ties her cardigan around her waist.

I like the way she looks with those bulky blue sleeves hugging her.
When she doesn't take the turn to her house, I ask what's up.
"I thought you said the party was at four."

"It is, but I have to pick up Baba's present at Mr. Togo's."

Mr. Togo is our school gardener, and he lives a few blocks past
Rosey's street. "You're giving her flowers?" Somehow I thought she
would make a bigger deal of her grandmother's present. I remember
the beautiful silk dress Baba gave her on her sixteenth birthday. It
has a high collar and buttons that look like rosebuds. It's pale blue,
and makes Rosey look like one of those soft-skinned, smiling women
you see in ads for Japan Air. The ads that make you want to run
out and buy a ticket right away even if you can't afford it and you
never thought of flying to Asia before.

"Not exactly flowers," Rosey says. "Come on, I'll show you."
We cross the street to the house and push open the basement door
without knocking. A bell rings somewhere in the back, and Mrs.
Togo comes out.

Mrs. Togo isn't anything like her lean, muscular husband. She
looks old enough to be his mother, even though her hair is still dark.
But she smells good, bringing the juicy, clean scent of grapefruit
into the room with her.

"Have you got the tree for Baba?" Rosey asks.

"Tree?" First, I thought Rosey was giving too small a present.
Now I've changed my mind. "Rose, we can't get a tree all the way
to your house."

Mrs. Togo smiles. "You can carry this one." She disappears,
then comes back with a small turquoise dish in her hand. It's the
size of a sardine can, but there's a tree growing in it. A gnarled,
twisted tree with a fat trunk and a halo of sharp, green needles. It's
all bent to one side, as if the wind had turned it into a waterfall.

"Amazing!" I can't take my eyes off the tiny tree. It looks hundreds of years old, yet it's only about eight inches high.

"This is bonsai," Mrs. Togo says. She holds the dish toward me, and I'm breathing in the sap, sweet and sticky.

"Did Mr. Togo grow this?"

The little woman laughs. "He helped. It has taken the lifetimes of three men to grow this juniper."

"Get down here." Suddenly Rosey is squatting on the floor and looking up at the tree. I feel pretty dumb, but I do it too.

When I look up from the moss-covered roots of the juniper into its branches, it's as if I've shrunk, as if I'm lying on my back under the shadow of a huge tree.

"This is the best way to look at bonsai," Rosey says. "Mr. Togo has dozens, and he made me kneel down and check each one. I picked this 'cause it made me dizzy when I looked up."

I don't say anything. I just take Rosey's hand until we're both inches high, small enough to fit inside a dollhouse. I have this weird feeling now, this fear of standing up again. I don't want to go back to being big. I want the two of us to stay here forever in this miniature, perfect world.

But Rosey breaks the spell, yanking my hand and pulling me up. She thanks Mrs. Togo, lets her slip a dark plastic bag over the juniper, and we head back out to the street. All the way to her house, Rosey's talking about the party, about the food her mother's made, but I'm in this dreamy sort of envelope where I only half hear her. In my head, I'm on my back, stretched across dark, springy moss, staring up through twisted branches at a cloudless sky.

5

"What if it's the same as it was with Mom?" Franklin had grabbed the brass fish, but now he replaced it silently, without knocking on the Mishimis' door. He'd dreaded this moment the whole six blocks to their house. "What if your folks can't see you? What if they don't believe me?"

"I told you," Rosey said. "I've got to try." Her face was rigid, expressionless, as if she were holding herself in check.

Above them, a glass wind chime stuttered faintly as it spun. Franklin felt the breeze on his neck but noticed how Rosey's hair remained unruffled, still. Had it blown behind her in the car because he remembered it that way? "I just don't want you to be hurt, is all."

Rosey's butterfly rash was spreading across her cheeks. "What about my *parents*, Lin? Don't you think *they've* been hurt? Don't you think *they've* suffered, too?" The stiff mask of her face crumpled for a minute, and a glimmer, like tears, rimmed her eyes.

Franklin sighed, picked up the knocker again. He hammered against the door only once before Mrs. Mishimi opened it. She looked smaller than he remembered, not as old as Baba, but tired. The shadows under her eyes were dark as bruises. Still, she smiled when she saw who it was. "Franklin!" She repeated his name as if it were a charm, something to ward off whatever had been bothering her. "Franklin! What a nice surprise."

"Mom?" Rosey sounded timid, younger. "Mom, it's me."

"Come in." Mrs. Mishimi invited Franklin without looking at her daughter. She led him to a pair of small chairs, beside a cream-colored screen in the far corner of the living room. He glanced around the lovely, austere room. Then the two of them sat awkwardly on the silk chairs, smiling, silent.

There was no chair for Rosey. Franklin thought of getting up, but the old fear was there. The fear of making an issue, of bringing things to a head. Besides, Rosey clearly wanted to stay near her mother. Her mask slipping again, fighting for control, she reached for Mrs. Mishimi's hands, and Franklin felt himself tense as her long fingers slid like light off the older woman's lap. "Tell her, Lin," Rosey commanded. "Tell her now."

He knew how it would go, but he sighed, then delivered the message. "Mrs. Mishimi," he said, "Rosey's here with us. She wants you to know she loves you."

Mrs. Mishimi stopped smiling and started kneading her sweater. She began at the bottom, near the last button, her nervous fingers pulling, pinching. "I've never doubted Rosey loved us," she said. "Tell me, now. How are you doing? How's school?"

"Okay, I guess." He watched her fingers, long and delicate like Rosey's, dance toward the next button, grab it, and twist fiercely. "What I mean is, Rosey is standing next to you right now."

Mrs. Mishimi winced as if she'd been slapped, and let go of the button. She stared at him, almost harshly. "Franklin, we all wish that were true." She shattered Rosey into motes now, into beams of light, as she leaned across to touch his hand. "But wishing won't bring her back."

"Yes, it can, Mom." Restored, Rosey knelt beside Mrs. Mishimi, and tried to force herself into her mother's line of sight. "I heard Lin crying. And here I am."

It wasn't exactly guilt, the small itch Franklin felt when she said it. More like the surprise when you turn a corner and walk toward a mirror. Had he made the miracle?

"Why not let things alone, go on with your life?" Mrs. Mishimi urged. "I know that's what she would want."

"I want you to hear me," Rosey told her, her voice hoarse, throaty with checked sobs. "I want you to look at me, that's what I want."

But all her mother saw—Franklin was an expert at reading between patient words, at deciphering vague, indulgent smiles—was a young boy swamped by grief, a romantic kid denying what someone older, someone used to disappointment, could accept.

Rosey's father saw the same thing. When he joined them a few minutes later, Harold Mishimi tried to be gentle. "I know how you feel, Franklin," he said. "I didn't want to believe it, either. My little girl—" He stopped, like a weight lifter at the top of a push, then rushed on. "Our Rosey was one of a kind. We'll never forget her, son."

"Dad." Rosey said it without hope, a sorrowful, almost soundless exhalation that made Franklin want to weep. Desperate, petitionary, she touched her father's shoulder with her useless, light-splashed fingers, brushed his cheek with her hand.

"But you can't freeze time. You can't keep the good moments and pretend the bad ones never happened." Mr. Mishimi pushed his glasses up the bridge of his nose to stare sternly, mournfully, at Franklin. "Listen," he added, relenting. "Why don't you and I take in a Nets game sometime? My office has season tickets, and there are always extras."

The two of them had never spent more than a few minutes together. Franklin, who was pretty sure Mr. Mishimi was no great basketball fan, nodded. "That'd be great, sir," he said. "Just great."

"Baba," Rosey demanded suddenly. "I want to see Baba."

Two down, one to go. The worst was over, and Franklin had nothing to lose. "Where's your mother, sir? Could we . . . could I talk to her?"

"O-ba-san?" Mr. Mishimi glanced at his wife. "I'm sure she'd love to see you, Franklin. But she's pretty ill. She's been in bed for a week. I think it would be best if you—"

"You make my mind up?" The question came from down the hall. "I think before you breathe, *gaki*. I still think good."

"Mama, I only meant—" Mr. Mishimi colored, smiled.

"Company help," Baba insisted. "I tired your face, anyway. Let him come."

"Just for a minute," Mrs. Mishimi said. "She gets exhausted. You know the way?" She looked down the hall toward Baba's tiny room.

Franklin nodded, glanced at Rosey, then led the way. Peering into the room, he saw Rosey's grandmother in the middle of a huge teak bed, the carved bridal bed she'd brought with her from Japan seventy years ago. She appeared to be floating on an island of asparagus-colored silk sheets and thick green blankets. Beside her, on a small table, was the bonsai juniper.

"Come," she urged, as soon as Franklin's head appeared in her door frame. "I no bite. I no—"

Her eyes widened, and something tender, watery, happened to her mouth. "Hana-chan!" She held her arms open. "Hana-chan, you come back!" Rosey rushed to the bed and nuzzled gratefully against the old woman's violet bed jacket. She turned into light, fluttered away, just as she always did when she touched someone. But Baba didn't seem to notice. Instead, she held tight to the dancing, sunlit air.

"Oh, Baba, it's so good to see you." His girl sounded giddy with relief, and Franklin felt the doubt flow out of him like water tumbling downhill. He hadn't conjured Rosey up, hadn't imagined her. Not if Baba saw her too.

"What's all this about your being sick?" Rosey straightened to examine her grandmother. "You look wonderful."

Baba pulled herself up, her leathery face tightening with pride. "I no sick. I dying."

"What?" Franklin came closer, thinking he'd heard the old woman wrong.

"I no sick one day in life," Baba insisted. "Take good care. Now over, that all."

She said it so matter-of-factly, so simply, Franklin wondered if she'd begun to lose her faculties, go a little soft in the head.

"Baba, I'm all mixed up," Rosey said. "I wanted to come home, and I didn't. I'm so tired, but Lin was crying." She darted a look at Franklin, a mild, accusatory glance.

"Old ones should go first, show way." Baba sighed. "Hard when young go before old. Very hard."

"Can you tell them, Baba?" Rosey sat on the bed beside her grandmother. "Can you tell Mom and Dad I'm back?"

The old woman turned from her granddaughter, stared at the small, gnarled tree in its turquoise dish. Franklin, following her glance, was amazed to see clusters of tiny blue berries sprouting from almost every branch. "I can tell, yes," she said. "But cannot make believe. Who believe old woman? Old woman with mind that wander?"

The pastel room, its silk and lace, its smell of incense, changed, grew suddenly brittle, when Harold Mishimi appeared at the door. "Mama," he said. "We don't want to tire you out. You've got to save your energy."

"Save for what? Don't need be strong to die."

"Mama-san," Mr. Mishimi scolded. "Nobody's dying. You've got years left."

Baba shrugged, smiled at her granddaughter. "Go now. I see you soon."

"Promise, O-ba?" Rosey stood but hovered uncertainly by the bed. "Maybe I should stay."

"You can't stay," Baba told her. "You go with him." She nodded at Franklin.

Mr. Mishimi grinned, glad to be getting his way so easily. "See?" he said to Franklin, leading the way back down the hall. "Sometimes my mother actually listens to me."

"I love you, Baba." Rosey followed reluctantly, walking backward out of the room. "Don't forget I love you."

Franklin shook hands with the Mishimis in the living room. "We're so glad you stopped by," Rosey's mother said. "I hope you'll feel free to visit anytime you need to."

Rosey wore a tight, small smile, the mildest of storm warnings. She watched her parents solemnly. "I wish I were as brave as they are," she said. "I wish I could make sense of this."

"Don't worry," Franklin told her before he could stop himself. "We still have each other."

"Well," Mrs. Mishimi answered, sounding surprised. "I guess we do, Franklin. Thank you."

The breeze had died to fits and starts by the time they'd left. The wind chime on the porch was spinning silently, its glass pendants passing each other without touching. *We're like that*, Franklin thought, watching his girl, wondering if the visit had been worth it. *So close, without being able to touch.*

Rosey's slender back was stiff, rigid with regret, as she turned at the bottom of the steps and doubled back around the house. He followed, watched her steal through a bare, low-slung hedge, then walk to the living room window. Halfway across the yard, he saw her press her hands against the frame, lean in close to the glass.

When she turned and started toward him, Franklin felt

ashamed, as if he'd been spying. He whirled around, stood rooted to the spot, pretending to have waited for her there. But all the way home, he pictured that window in his mind— the small invisible print of a ghost kiss and the Mishimis moving back and forth behind it, never knowing.

6

Archmont High. For six months the sight of its pseudo-Victorian turrets, its sprawling brick additions, had filled Franklin with dread. Walking down the crowded hallways, he'd felt alone, hollow as a dried-out gourd. Navigating the tunnels and crannies that led from basement chem labs to the offices, from third-floor classes to the cafeteria, had been like opening sore after sore. Everyplace he looked, each corner he turned, there was a memory.

And so he had gradually stopped going. He tried to show up for tests, a few football games, but more and more he had stayed in bed. Every morning his mother had opened his door and addressed the stubborn mound of blankets and sheets in the center of his bed. "Franklin," she'd said, "did you push the snooze button again? You're going to be late."

And every morning he'd rolled over, stretched, and found not a single reason to get up. Only the old emptiness. A pain under his rib cage, as if he were a deep-sea diver decompressing. It hardly seemed worth walking to school, groggy and aching; watching the clock crawl through math, then lunch, then science. Then what? None of it mattered.

But not today. Today, when he opened his eyes, when he found Rosey pacing the room waiting for him to wake up, the pain was gone. And so were all his negative feelings about Archmont. In fact, he felt downright nostalgic about the old place. He couldn't wait for the two of them to go back there together.

But Rosey was in no hurry. "Things are different now," she insisted. "I'm different."

"No, you're not." No more wandering the halls, no more going through the motions. "And we're not either, Rose. We're the same as ever. You'll see."

But his enthusiasm wasn't enough to persuade her. Her bottom lip lost its firmness, got wavery, and turned in on itself. Her eyes went uncertain too. "I can't," she told him. "I just can't."

Franklin had seen Rosey angry and hurt; he'd known her to be childish, happy, sly. But somehow, it had never occurred to him she could be afraid. "Hey," he said, wanting to hold her, stroke her hair. "Hey, Mishimi." His voice was hoarse, broken with love. "Are you going soft on me?"

"It feels like when I tried to squeeze into that velvet skirt I loved in junior high." Her eyes told him there was more to this, something bigger than she could put into words. "I knew the waist would be too small, I knew the zipper wouldn't close, but I kept remembering how great it had looked, what a good time I'd had wearing it."

"I've already missed so many days of school, I might not graduate." He hated himself for blaming her, for trying to make her feel guilty.

"Going back won't work, Lin-lin. We can't." She looked baffled, cornered. "Last night, while you were asleep, I started thinking about the others, the ones who are waiting for me. I was coming close to them, reaching out." Now, her tone told him, it was his turn to feel guilty. "But then you dreamed about me, and it all got wiped away."

"Last night?" He couldn't recall a single dream. He'd slept hard and deep, as if he were making up for months of insomnia, the chain of dawns that had found him ragged, defeated, before he'd even begun.

"All I could see, all I could feel, were the pictures in your mind. Pictures of us."

For an instant, a runaway second, Franklin felt responsible, wrong. But then her white neck, her mahogany eyes, her dear, dreamed-of voice overwhelmed everything else. "I want you to come to classes with me." He lowered his head, looked at her from under the lock of hair that had fallen in front of his eyes. "Like old times. Please?"

When she sighed and fell into step beside him, color rushed back into his world. For the last six months he'd lived in a vague, dreary vacuum. Going to the store, driving, meeting friends at Pizzeria Presto—had all taken such effort, like wading through solid, gray chunks of time. But now, as he gulped the orange juice his mother had left on the kitchen counter, pocketed a doughnut, and walked outside with Rosey, Franklin was astounded at how bright and sharp everything looked.

The leafless trees, their scrawny branches cutting into the clear sky, amazed him. The neon ski jackets of the students they passed, the flaming orange running suit of an early-morning jogger who flashed by, the cars snaking along in rush-hour formation, were as varied, as rich, as flowers. Flowers in February!

As they neared the school, the Easter-basket green of Archmont's AstroTurf football field seemed vibrant, full of promise. "The lacrosse team is going to use the new field this spring," he told Rosey, waving toward the precisely lined rectangle inside the oval track. "Even before the Almighty Arrows sink their cleats into it."

For the first time since the field had been finished behind schedule last fall, Franklin was excited at the prospect of playing on it. He pictured bright, square-shouldered numbers popping into life on the new digital scoreboard. He heard an imaginary announcer tell the stands, "And that's another score for middie Franklin Sanders. There's no stopping number thirty-eight today, is there?"

He remembered now how good it felt, the sharp, condensed plunk of the ball landing in his stick, the way it spun and pressed against the pocket as he cradled it, just before he sent it flying. The smell of his own sweat, the lime from the field, came back to him.

"Hey, Sand Man!"

When he turned his head, he was still running toward the goal, the world sliced in half by the face guard on his helmet, the crowd on their feet.

"Lin!" Loping toward Franklin, his long hair and awkward

gait unmistakable even at a distance, Dud waved wildly. He'd covered half the distance from the light at the corner, but he kept jogging, yelled again, flashing some sort of intricate code with his hands.

Franklin, his daydream gone, tried to decipher his friend's signals, shook his head, then turned back to Rosey. She had changed in the second he'd watched the field, or rather the light around her had. Her features, even her dark hair, had lost substance, had been swallowed up in the bright sun.

"Rose!" He reached out, forgetting for the umpteenth time that she was unreachable. He blinked, stared into the starchy light, straining to see her face.

"Wow!" she said. "That was an exciting game."

"What game?" A nameless inkling, a suspicion he didn't want to consider, fluttered into his consciousness, then got pushed away. Slowly the light around Rosey dimmed, and she gained dimension again, heft. "What are you talking about?"

"I'm talking about that lacrosse game you were playing in your head just now." Her smile faded, turned into a question as Dud, out of breath, pulled up beside them.

"Lin, for crying out loud!" Dud nodded, brows raised, at the clusters of students walking past them toward the huge, ungainly building. "Unless you want everyone here to figure you're finally running on empty, maybe you'd better talk to me"—he eyed the empty space next to Franklin—"instead of—"

"A nonexistent nobody?" Rosey finished. "A phantom without an opera?"

"Hey, he didn't mean it," Franklin soothed. Her anger, her

confusion, caused a shimmering that made her fade again. He focused on her outline, a snow white vacancy like an overexposed photo.

"Yes, he did." She refused to be comforted.

"Yes, I did," Dud insisted. "I'm serious, Lin." He glanced again at the students. Some were yelling across the quad; others were grabbing a final cigarette before the bell; Hughey Fine was doing his usual balancing act on top of the stair rail. "*I* already know you're crazy. But there's not much percentage in broadcasting it, is there?"

Franklin knew the path of least resistance when it was offered. And suddenly he was happy to take it. To let the matter drop. To forget about what had happened out there by the field. To walk with Dud up the steps; to high-five Hughey; to ask Charlie Strand how it was hanging; to feel a little like his old self. Because Rosey was still with him, because he kept her constantly in view.

Even after the second bell rang and Dud headed upstairs to bio, Franklin didn't take his eyes off his girl. All the way down the hall through the dense macaroni-and-cheese smell from the cafeteria, past the glass display case featuring Famous Firsts, beyond the clatter of keyboards in the computer lab, to the third locker from the end on the left-hand side.

He had promised her things would be the way they used to be. But he hadn't counted on Rosey herself being so different. She wasn't rushing along beside him with that beautiful dance-walk of hers, waving and gossiping, taking two short steps to every one of his. Instead she was moving slowly, noiselessly, down the tile corridor, without footsteps or words. She stared around her, as if Archmont were all new, a curious, foreign place to which she had only the slimmest connection. Until they stopped at his locker.

Her eyes rounded suddenly to glossy marbles. "Oh, my God, Lin, why didn't you tell me?" She stared in horror at the locker next to his.

"What?"

"Why didn't you tell me they gave my locker to Francie Travers?"

"How'd you know?"

"Who else would decorate their combination lock with pompoms?" She backed away from the offending white-and-gold tufts. "God, Lin, I think I'm going to barf. Do ghosts barf?"

He laughed. "A, you're not a ghost." He popped his own lock, then dumped half his books onto the bottom shelf of the locker. "And B, Francie Travers has been pretty great."

"Thanks." He turned, found himself face-to-face with his class's student congress delegate, the second runner-up for Archmont homecoming queen, and cocaptain of the school's cheerleading squad.

Francie stood beside him, or rather up against him, crowding him toward his locker. She was pretty in a scrubbed, uncomplicated way, and brimming with sympathy. "I know what it's like to lose someone you love," she said, her face turned to his like a sunflower. "I thought I'd never get over it when Roger dumped me."

He didn't bother to point out that she and Roger had dated for only a few months, or that her ex-boyfriend was attending classes at Amherst and still, so far as anyone knew, very much alive. Francie was prone to exaggeration. Everything she did and said was bigger than life. The whole school had watched, as if at a movie, when she'd suffered her first romantic rejection. "I wouldn't mind if I'd kissed a frog," she'd told anyone who would listen, "and he'd turned into a prince. But it's not supposed to happen the other way round. That's just not fair, is it?"

Now she covered Franklin's hand with her own, her eyes as deep, as unbelievably blue, as new denim. "If there's anything I can do," she said, "don't you dare be afraid to ask."

"Nice contacts." Without turning, he knew Rosey was making her lemon-tasting face. Or sticking her finger down her throat. "I wouldn't count on the hair being natural, either."

"Seriously," Francie insisted, her hand lingering on his, "I want you to know you're not alone with this. I'm here for you."

"That's great." He shifted the books in his arms, slipping his hand away. "But I'm fine."

"For real?" Francie looked suddenly brighter, more like the girl who stood behind the grandstand every fall, begging the crowd to give her an A. "Well, that's terrific. 'Cause I was thinking maybe, I mean, since we have so much in common and all—" She stopped, smiling up at him. "You know."

"My mother's uncle's half sister," Rosey announced, "knew a saying that fits this occasion perfectly—"

"There's no point in wasting the best years of our lives, is there?" Francie fell into step beside Franklin, who made sure Rosey flanked him on the other side, then hurried toward room 305 and the English test he was already late for.

"Don't you have a class now?" he asked Francie.

"A samurai sworn to chastity," Rosey continued, "will be compelled to defend himself against the attacks of hungry women long before he will need to draw his sword in battle."

She's jealous, it occurred to him. *Rosey's actually jealous.* It amused him and staggered him at once. Could she have mismeasured his love that much? Didn't she know what she meant to him?

"No, I have a free period." Francie stopped just outside the classroom door. "Want to have lunch later?"

"I am *not* jealous," Rosey insisted. "Still, I think the least you could do is tell her you're sworn to chastity."

"I can't," Franklin said.

"Why not?" Francie asked.

"Why not?" Rosey wanted to know.

"Because I've got to study." He picked up his science book, waving it in Francie's direction. "I've really been letting things slip."

"But it's senior year. Nobody studies senior year."

"Maybe another time, okay?" He peered through the glass panel in the door to 305. The whole class was silent, heads bent over their papers. "Gotta go."

A few students looked up as he took the sheet Ms. Westerman handed him, twisted in their seats as he found an empty desk at the back of the room, then turned back to their own tests when he started reading quietly.

Instructions
This test will consist of ONE ESSAY, covering both books you've read this semester: Compare and contrast the

treatment of the theme of alienation in Ralph Ellison's INVISIBLE MAN and Saul Bellow's THE DANGLING MAN. Discuss the content and structure of these novels, as well as your personal response to each author's voice.

The second book was short; Franklin had read it months ago in a kind of stupor, one of Rosey's Chuck Berry albums blasting away in the background. He'd liked Ellison's novel, though, he was sure of that. At the moment, however, he couldn't remember why. What he did remember, what suddenly frightened him, was what Rosey had told him a few minutes ago. She had said she wasn't jealous. But how had she known that was what he'd been thinking?

The words in front of him blurred, ran together. *You've read alienation INVISIBLE DANGLING.* If Rosey could read his thoughts, did that mean he was making her up, after all? Baba was an old woman, an old woman who loved Rosey almost as much as he did. Had they dreamed her together? Was she simply a creation of their longing? *Discuss your personal voice.* Maybe Stiller was right. Maybe Franklin was crazy.

Allow ten minutes for planning and outlining your response. Take 20 minutes to write your two- to three-page essay. Reserve ten minutes for CAREFUL PROOFING. You will be judged on your grasp of both the material <u>and</u> the rules of grammar!

He was afraid to think about the test, afraid to concentrate on anything but Rose. He glanced at his girl, who had walked to one of the windows that ran the width of the room. He was reassured by the way she stood there, arms folded, staring solemnly out toward the parking lot. *Careful.* But she had nearly disappeared when he'd thought about lacrosse. What would happen if he let his guard down, if he forgot to remember? *You will be judged on your grasp.* It didn't matter, Franklin decided, whether he'd willed her back, trapped her somehow in his fierce yearning. What did matter, what filled him with energy and determination and a gratitude close to tears, was the glorious fact of her return. If it meant failing this test, failing a thousand bazillion tests, it didn't matter. He'd wrap his heart and mind around her so tightly, she'd never fade again. *The rules.* He had to. He couldn't bear to let her go.

July, the middle of the month

Ever since she got fired from the Elite Dress Shop, Rosey's been desperate for a new job. She says Mrs. Maynard at Elite is as close to being a witch as you can get without taking courses. She says to tell my mother that before a sale, Mrs. Maynard makes up "suggested retail prices" so everything looks like a bargain. She says that if she doesn't find another job quick, she'll never save enough for the dress she wants to wear to my cousin's wedding.

"Wait 'til you see it, Lin." Rosey is modeling the dress already, turning as if she were on a runway. "Pink, but not obnoxious, It's-a-Girl pink." She twirls toward me. Her hair's grown long again, and it lifts just a little when she spins, one hand on her waist. "More of a light mauve."

"Mauve?" I bet she could be a real model if she wanted. Still, I always think of her as a dancer. She's got the smallest feet I've ever seen on someone over six, and she moves the way a flower would if it could walk.

"A purply pink," she explains. "The color of Baba's snapdrag-ons." She stops whirling, pulls out the front of her T-shirt, making sharp points next to her breasts. "And it's got this low neckline that sort of pushes me up, gives me, you know, great boobs."

I laugh, but then I swallow hard, remembering what Rosey looks like under her T. "You already have great boobs," I tell her. Small and round, so white you can see her veins. Like china. Like a white porcelain dish with the sun shining through it.

I want to pull her to me, slip my hands under her shirt, kiss her neck. But we're standing in the kitchen of her house. We can hear her mother's vacuum cleaner in the living room. And Baba's sewing machine down the hall. I settle for a quick hug.

She grabs the keys to the Bubble Gum Machine off one of the hooks by the door. "Come on. Let's go land me that job. You've been paying our way all summer."

We head out to the garage. "That's what guys are supposed to do," I tell her. "Open doors. Buy dinner. Stuff like that."

"Oh, God, Lin. Please!" Rosey pushes the door opener, then slips behind the wheel. I jump in beside her. "Are you talking about dating? Do you actually think you and I go on dates?"

I've never thought of Rosey as a date. She's Rosey. My Rose. That's all. I guess she feels the same. "So what is it we do?" I ask.

"We're together," she says. She slips her hand in mine, and the Bubble Gum Machine lurches out of the driveway. "I mean, we just are. And when one of us carries all the weight, it sort of spoils that." She fishes in the backpack she's thrown on the floor, comes out with a pair of sunglasses, new ones I've never seen before. "It feels like we're not partners, you know? That's why I want this scooper job so much."

I found the ad yesterday. It's for a counterperson at Sundaes

Unlimited, the new ice cream place that opened off Route 49. The pay is better than Rosey was making at Elite, and the hours would work, even once school starts. "Maybe I should apply too," I tell her, only half joking. "We could scoop together."

She turns to face me for a second, then looks back at the road. She's put on the sunglasses, and they're much too big for her. She looks like the spoiled bad girl in one of those dumb college movies. The ones where no one studies because they're too busy going to frat parties and keeping track of who's in bed with who.

"But you already have a great job at the Tempo." She turns off the highway toward Sundaes. It's a round building, painted white except for a big chocolate roof that drips down between the windows and doors. "I thought you loved doing those articles," she says.

"They're not really articles," I say. "And I'm not really a Tempo reporter. I just sit around at different town meetings and take notes. Or run down to the police station. Most of the time, someone else writes the story."

"Police station?" Rosey opens her door, gets out. "You didn't tell me you get to go to the police station."

"Yeah." I have to slide over to her side to get out because she's parked too close to a dark green, high-finish Lexus. "I pick up the blotter; it lists all the arrests for each week."

"I always wondered what happens when people go to jail." I can tell she's nervous about getting the job. She's free-associating, and she's talking a mile a minute. "Like what happens if they live alone, have no friends?"

"Haven't you watched prison movies?" I ask her. "They get sent up, and they have murderers as cell mates and have to give a carton of cigarettes to the prison bully every week."

"No." She's stalling, standing by the main entrance, letting other people in. "I don't mean what happens to them. I mean what happens to their pets? Who feeds a cat if its master gets sent away for years or something? Who takes a dog for walks? Who even knows they exist?"

Leave it to Rosey to worry about that. "I don't know," I tell her. "I never thought about it." Which is strange, actually, since I've got Mingo, and the Mishimis don't even own a pet.

Rosey's still considering this, her head at an angle, her new sunglasses slipped to the bottom of her nose. I wait until a whole family has trooped in, four or five little kids scooting under their parents' arms. Then I open the glass door and bow. "After you, madam." I figure she'll only come up with another problem if we don't get this interview over with.

She takes a big breath, pushes up her glasses, and walks inside. There's a circular counter in the center of the place, with all the tables and chairs set up around it. The people sitting at the tables have two options: They can look out the windows at the parking lot and the highway traffic, or they can watch the kids behind the counter packing cones and making sundaes.

The whole place has this dizzy, syrupy smell like you're going to drown in sugar. There's a sign hanging over the counter with a big color photo of ice cream, scoops and scoops of it, all strung out in a parade of yellow and lime and pink and chocolate balls. The smell and the photo make me think of something my mother says sometimes: Too much of a good thing.

The kids working here are wearing big blue chef's aprons and these dorky blue-and-white-checked hats. The girls (there are two of them, moving back and forth, up and down, fast as an old-time movie) look all right in these outfits; the boys (three, one with long hair tied back in a ponytail) look dumb, and they know it. Their faces are all tight, their noses and mouths pinched together over the deep aluminum tubs of ice cream. No one looks up when we walk over. Every table is full, and there's a line of people a zillion miles long waiting to place orders.

"It says to see the manager." Rosey has pulled the ad out of her backpack. She studies the craziness behind the counter. "So where is he?"

We get on the end of a smaller line by the cash register. When we've moved to the front, Rosey asks the boy who holds out his hand for our check where the manager is.

"Oh." The boy puts his hand down, closes the register drawer. "You both here about the job?"

"Just me." Rosey takes off her sunglasses. "Who do I talk to?"

"Will's right over there." The boy points behind the counter to a girl washing scoops in a big metal tub. She's small, doesn't look like she's out of high school yet. And she sure doesn't look like anyone called Will.

It turns out her real name is Willow. "My folks are nature freaks," she explains. "Really into trees." She smiles, and I notice that what looked like a birthmark on her chin is actually a spot of raspberry sherbet. "I've got a brother named Ash and a sister, Magnolia."

"That's nice," Rosey tells her. "Willow's nice."

"Yeah, I guess," the girl says. "Could be worse." She grins. "Ginkgo or something!"

"Or Bald Cypress," I volunteer. My dad's kind of an outdoor type, so I know enough flora and fauna to get by. "Or Horse Chestnut." Both girls are looking at me like I'm nuts. "Or—"

"I'm here about the job," Rosey says.

"Great!" Willow snaps into business mode right away. "Can you start today?"

"Are you serious?" Rosey looks around the busy room, then back at Willow.

"Look, I just had two people call in sick." Willow has blond hair and eyes that match her apron. I figure from the take-charge sound of her voice that maybe she's in college, after all. "We're really going crazy here. Can you do it?"

"Sure, I'd like to." Rosey lets my hand go, watches the jerky movements of the kids behind the counter. "But I've never done this sort of work before. I mean, I don't even know where stuff is."

"That's okay." Willow leaves the scoops in the tub, opens a tiny door built into the counter, and comes out to stand beside us. "Come on. I'll get you a uniform, and you can train with me." She grins past Rosey at me. "How about you, Mr. Tree?" she asks. "Want a job, too?"

I think about the blue cap and the apron. I think about the library council meeting I'm supposed to be covering in exactly thirty minutes. It's gotten so they save a seat for me, put out a Coke instead of a coffee. "No, thanks," I tell her. "Not right now. Maybe later."

Willow shrugs. "No harm in asking, right?" She takes a look at the two of us, the way Rosey's stepped back against me, taken my hand again. "She'll be done by six. Think you can last 'til then?" She thinks she's pretty tough, pretty funny. I like her.

Willow turns and heads for a white door in the back wall. Rosey stuffs her glasses in her backpack and looks at me, rolling her eyes. "That was easy," she whispers, then tosses me the keys to the jeep. "See you at six."

As I leave, pushing open the glass door, letting still more customers in, I'm not sorry I turned down the job offer. I breathe the air outside; it's hot and damp, working itself up to rain. But it smells wonderful after the sticky sweetness inside. Rosey and I will have plenty of time together, I tell myself. The rest of our lives, in fact. Maybe we'll even start our own business someday.

Mishimi-Sanders. I say it inside my head as I'm climbing into the jeep. Mishimi-Sanders, Inc., Purveyors of fine what? What could we make? I turn the ignition on, and the radio starts up. Rosey loves music, I think. And I love to write. Maybe I'll write songs, and Rosey could put the lyrics to music. Singing Fools. That's it, that's much better. Recorded at Singing Fools Studio. Maybe I'll dig out some of those old poems after the meeting. Singing Fools, Inc. I can't wait to tell Rosey.

7

"Look over there." After school, they'd left by the back door because Franklin wanted to do two things. One, avoid Francie. Two, show Rosey what her friends had done. "See? That garden with the sundial?"

Rosey nodded.

"It was donated by our class. And there's a rosebush with a plaque and your name on it." He glanced at the bush, which had been trimmed back to a few naked, budless stumps. "Of course, it's nothing much to see right now. But this summer—"

He realized how barren the spot must look, a neat rectangle of cleared dirt, a copper sundial catching the dwindling afternoon sun. "They asked me to write a poem for the plaque. I tried, Rose." Each time he'd sharpened his pencils and sat down to the task, he'd written only a few lines before crumpling the paper. "I couldn't do it."

He'd always written, even when he was little. He'd always loved the look of an empty page, the excitement of picking up a pencil to fill it. He'd written journals and scrapbooks, sci-fi epics, short stories, newspaper articles, and about eight notebooks full of poems. These last had endeared him to his English teachers but had also made him the butt of some pretty stupid jokes from his teammates on the lacrosse team. "Who cares?" Rosey had told him. "They're just jealous. Dylan is a rock poet. You're a jock poet. It could be worse."

And now, of course, he knew she was right—it could be much worse. Since the accident last summer, he'd hardly written a word. Certainly not about Rosey. Sure, he'd kept the journal for Dr. Stiller, but that was different. It was a way of going back, of keeping things the way they were. To write about her death, though, to pen some sappy tribute so everyone could forget, could leave her behind, that was something he would never do.

"So the plaque is kind of plain; just your name and—" He paused, tried to find her eyes, but she had knelt down beside the bare bush. "And the dates. Is that okay?"

"What color are they?" She looked up at him. "The roses?"

"Yellow, I think." He'd stood with Rosey's grandmother and the Mishimis at the brief ceremony. Numb, claustrophobic, he'd barely glanced at the plant. "Your mom called them tea roses." He remembered the overwhelming heat, the pressure of the tears building like an ocean behind a dike. He remembered being surprised by the number of people who'd packed themselves into the small grassy square, some of them not even from school.

Mrs. Maynard from the dress shop had come, had shaken

hands with the Mishimis and Baba, then smiled gingerly at Franklin, as if she didn't know what to make of him. He'd been caught off guard by how soft, how genteel and ravaged, her face had looked—nothing like the ogre out of Rosey's horror stories. Two of the families Rosey used to baby-sit for, including a baby in a stroller and an itchy little toddler in a floppy, genderless pair of overalls, stayed toward the back and left when the baby began to scream. And Willow from Sundaes Unlimited had been there too. Rosey's young "boss" had looked even smaller and blonder out of uniform than she had at work. She told Franklin that Rosey was beautiful inside and out, something that stuck in his mind longer than the endless speech Mr. Gerson, Archmont's principal, had given.

The heavy man, sweating in a dark suit, had talked on and on—about Rosey's academic record, her scientific flair, her "drive to succeed." After a while Franklin had closed down, shut out those useless words. If you strung them all together, he'd thought, all the kind, empty words, they still wouldn't reach his Rose.

Baba must have felt the same way, because after everyone had left, she stooped down from the waist, as if her knees were unbendable, and began digging around the base of the rosebush. Franklin and the Mishimis watched her, nonplussed. "What on earth are you doing, Mother?" Harold Mishimi asked at last.

"Need air. Packed too tight," Baba told him, pinching and sifting the soil around the thorny stem. She dug faster, more furious, until it looked as if she might unearth the whole bush. Finally Mrs. Mishimi took her mother-in-law's arm and gently lifted her upright, then walked her toward their car. It was only when they passed by Franklin that he saw the old woman was crying, that he realized he was, too.

But today there were no tears, no people, no pale flowers. There was only the rosebush, stuck like a bare sword in the earth, and Franklin wished he hadn't brought Rosey here. He'd meant to show her how much the school loved her, how much she was missed. Instead, the desolate spot had turned her somber, moody.

She rose to her feet, stared past the parking lot toward the school's turreted profile. "I wish I could remember what it was like to touch things," she said. Her voice was listless, small.

A crow called from an oak branch above the roseless bush. The wind tugged at the collar of Franklin's nylon jacket, and he watched without being able to help.

"I'd like to eat fries with mustard again, or cast a shadow, even catch a cold." She was focused on something beyond the school, something Franklin couldn't see. "It's like I'm stuck in an elevator between floors, and even if I pressed a button and the door opened, there'd be nothing there but empty space."

The sun was hidden now, dropped behind the phony widow's walk that ran along the outside of the school's top story. In the weak light Rosey was clearer, more defined, than she'd seemed all day. But something else was clear, too. No matter how much he wanted it, willed it, she couldn't come back. Not all the way.

He'd barely gotten his coat off, had just opened the refrigerator door, taken out an apple and a jar of mayonnaise, when his mother gave him the news.

"Dr. Stiller says he can fit you in again this week." As if it was something he'd been hoping for, a blue ribbon opportunity.

Franklin sighed. Not a small, resigned sigh, but a bigger-than-life, my-mother-is-impossible sigh. "I just saw Stiller." He remembered the carving board, put the apple and a seeded roll on top. "Why this emergency session?"

"Because you are undoubtedly, indisputably, completely whacko." Rosey's dark mood had lifted a bit. Maybe it was the prospect of watching him devour her all-time favorite sandwich, apple slices and tuna.

"It's just a follow-up," his mother assured him, all smiles. "You know, to make sure you don't slip back."

"Slip back to what?" He sliced the apple paper-thin, the way Rosey always had.

His girl leaned across the kitchen table from him, her long hair ending just above the glinting knife. "Are you sure that's enough mayo?" she asked. "It's no good unless it's really soggy."

"Maybe 'slip back' isn't quite right," his mother said. "Actually, Dr. Stiller used 'regress.'"

"Okay." He slathered on more mayo. "Regress to what?"

Helen Sanders sat down right where Rosey was perched, and for a second he saw his mother through Rosey. Like a double-exposed photograph. It was over as soon as Rosey moved, but he'd hated that fraction of a second when she dissipated, threatened to blink off like a weak light.

His mother saw his face. "It's not what you think," she said. "The Mishimis called me yesterday. They mentioned your visit, how you told them Rosey was with you."

"So?" He'd explained all that. He thought she'd understood.

"So they're a little worried. They're afraid you're not getting on with your life. They care about you." His mother always played things down, but Franklin could imagine Mrs. Mishimi's report. *Poor kid.* He'd heard it dozens of times, times when people thought he wasn't listening, wasn't watching. *Poor kid. He's not taking it well.*

How did you take it well, anyway? Why should you? He remembered a poem by Dylan Thomas. In the poem Thomas tells his father, a sick old man, to "rage, rage against the dying of the light." What would he tell Rosey, who'd liked french fries and kisses and who'd been young enough to live for years and years?

"On the other hand," his mother said, "Leonard tells me you're feeling much more positive about school. He just wants to check in with you. I made the appointment for Tuesday."

"That's tomorrow."

"I know." She nodded. "Right after school."

"We can't." *Slow down. Careful.* "I mean, I can't. I've got plans." He and Rosey at the falls. No picnic, maybe. It was too cold yet. But old times. They *could* go back, just the two of them.

His mother wasn't giving up. "Leonard says we shouldn't let this slide."

"Leonard?" Franklin felt as though he'd missed something important. He studied his mother, who was suddenly intrigued by the colored flecks embedded in the Formica tabletop. "You and Dr. Stiller are on a first-name basis?"

"Put the knife down, Lin," Rosey advised, smiling for the first time all afternoon. "You're much better off discussing this without a weapon in your hand."

For once, Franklin ignored his girl. Knife still poised over the open sandwich, he stared at his mother. "Mom?"

Helen Sanders blinked at the Formica.

"Is there something you're not telling me?"

"It's nothing. Really." There was a healthy color spreading up from his mother's neck to her cheeks. "We've just . . . seen each other a few times. That's all."

"Seen each other?" Franklin couldn't have scripted anything more preposterous. He watched his mother trace tiny, invisible symbols on the table with her fingernail, tried to imagine her in the same room with his taciturn, pompous shrink. "*Seen* each other?"

"That's a euphemism for dating, Lin." Rosey was clearly enjoying this. Franklin was not.

"You know," his mother said, ". . . socially."

Finally he put down the knife. "You can't." It was too ridiculous. "That's . . . that's conflict of interest. Or something." He closed the sandwich. "It must be illegal."

His mother smiled weakly. "Leonard says if he and I become involved, he'll—"

"Involved?" Franklin felt a combination of hysteria and revulsion wipe out what was left of his hunger. He stared blankly at the sandwich he'd hoped would boost Rosey's sagging spirits, the sandwich he'd been determined to wolf down while she enjoyed the feast vicariously. "Involved?!"

"Franklin." His mother looked directly at him now. She'd stopped smiling. He saw something he hadn't noticed before, something at the back of her eyes. "It's been years since your father and I got divorced." It wasn't exhaustion or sadness; he'd seen her look tired and sad lots of times over the last six months. This was different.

She put her hand on his. "Leonard thinks I'm interesting, attractive. And when I'm with him, I feel as if I am."

It was loneliness. His mother was lonely! Franklin remembered how he had cried when he found the jar of peanut butter Rosey had brought to his house the day before she died. It was weeks after the accident, and he'd gotten furious when he looked at the expiration date on the label, smashed the jar against the wall.

It wasn't the same with his mother and dad, he knew. After all, the fights had been pretty gruesome. And it wasn't as if his father was dead, either. He was still on the planet, still answered his phone and sent them dutiful postcards full of his slanted, tiny script. But one day Franklin had come home early, caught his mother crying in the bedroom, her head buried in one of his dad's shirts. You could be lonely for somebody, he guessed, even if they were still alive.

He stood up now, put his hands on his mother's shoulders. "I think you're interesting, too, Mom," he said. He studied her graying honey-colored hair, her large, delicate eyes. "And you're pretty hot for someone your age."

Rosey slapped her forehead and made a clucking sound with her tongue. Helen Sanders rolled her eyes. "Thanks," she said. "I guess."

"What?" He looked at both the women he loved. They wore identical expressions, fond, quizzical. "What did I say?"

That night was full of dreams he remembered. Mainly because he kept waking up to make sure Rosey was there. "Don't worry,

Lin-lin," she told him finally. "Where would I go?"

"What does it feel like when I'm asleep? When you're alone?' he asked.

"Like waiting," she said. "Like waiting behind a rice paper screen—Remember the one in our living room, Lin? How it lets the light through? And just behind it, someone's waiting for me, too. I can't really see them, only their shadow. But I know they're there, I can feel them."

"That's how I felt, Rose." Franklin sat up in bed, saw her shining in the dark. "That's how I felt before you came back!"

"I know," she told him.

"Rose?"

"Hmm."

"I don't want you to be unhappy."

"I know that, too, Lin-san." She settled soundlessly on the foot of his bed. "Now go to sleep."

He curled on his side so he could watch her. "I'm sorry we can't go to the waterfall tomorrow."

"We'll go another time." The moonlight through the blinds melted into her bright shadow, made her shoulders and face swim in light. "You wouldn't want to miss your date with Dr. Stiller."

"It's not *my* date I'm worried about." Franklin turned on his back, stared at the ceiling. "God," he said. "Would you believe my mother and my shrink?"

"Hey," she said, "free therapy for life." He felt rather than saw her smile. "I can't wait to see this guy."

"I can," he told her, yawning, fighting sleep. "Trust me, Doctor Doom could ruin anybody's day."

8

Tuesday did in fact get off to a bad start, though Dr. Stiller could hardly be blamed for Franklin's running late. Not just a few minutes late, but the sort of hopeless late that means you trip all over yourself trying to save time and just make things worse. He'd already burned one bagel, grabbed another, and jammed it into the toaster when the phone rang.

"I'll watch breakfast," Rosey ordered. "You get the phone."

It was Willow, from the ice cream place. "I'm glad your mom didn't answer," she told Franklin. "A seven-thirty wake-up call isn't usually a big crowd pleaser."

"Mom's already at work," he said. "Early shoots all week. What's up?"

"I hope you are, Mr. Tree." Willow laughed. "Thought you might need a ride to school."

Willow had been a regular caller since Rosey's funeral. Nothing soupy or sentimental, just friendly how's-it-going conversations once a week or so. A couple of times she'd made the same offer she was making today, telling him Sundaes was right up the highway, right on her way to work. So far, he'd refused. Being stuck without wheels (his mother said two blocks to the bus stop was nothing, and a gas guzzler was the last thing they could afford) in front of a college woman was a little embarrassing.

Today, though, it was either accept Willow's offer or forget first period. And Mr. Denito had made it clear that one more absence would put Franklin's sociology grade into the Twilight Zone. "Thanks," he said now. "I surfaced a little late. I could really use the lift."

Rosey, though, was shaking her head, gesturing like a drowning swimmer. Franklin put his hand on the phone, grinned. "Why not?" he asked, remembering Francie. "Jealous again, Mish?"

"Lin, who is that?"

"It's Willow Sloan, that's who."

"I thought so." Rosey stared at the portable phone in Franklin's hand. "Trust me, Lin. You really don't want to drive to school with Will."

He was tickled, flattered all over again. "You *are* jealous! Hey, she's a million years older than me!"

"Lin, I'm telling you—"

"Sorry, Rose. Desperate times." Franklin uncovered the phone, spoke into it. "Listen, Will," he said. "I'd really appreciate it." The second bagel, dark but not black, was stuck in the toaster. He dug it out with his free hand. "If you don't mind stopping by."

"On my way, Mr. Tree. See ya."

But Rosey didn't look jealous, after all. Just amused, foxy. "You didn't tell me you and Will were so tight."

"We're not." He smeared a film of grape jelly across his bagel, eyed the result, then devoured half in one bite. "She just calls to make sure I'm going to school, stuff like that."

"Will's not *that* old. Why is she playing Mommy?"

He grabbed his backpack from the counter. "She's not." They headed for the door, Franklin still holding what was left of his bagel in one hand. "Not exactly."

It was bright and cool outside, the kind of day his dad had liked best for hiking. Franklin could picture his father, eyes raised to the sky, breathing deeply and pronouncing, "Not too hot, not too cold." He sat on the front steps to wait for their ride, and Rosey stood above him.

"So how come you didn't tell me?" she persisted. "About you and Will?"

"There's nothing to tell. She just calls once in a while, that's all."

He wished he hadn't brought the bagel with him. He didn't feel hungry anymore. "Will had this other sister. Besides Magnolia, I mean." He swiveled on the step, looked up at his girl. "Didn't she ever tell you?"

Rosey shook her head.

"She was older, another tree name. I've forgotten just what." He looked away, stared into the street. "She died when Will was still in high school. She was really sick. It took a long time."

Rosey sat down beside him.

"Anyway, a couple of months ago, I began to feel like this

pathetic charity case," he explained. "You know, the way she kept calling, being nice?

"So I kind of yelled at her, and that's when she told me. Said she kept thinking about her sister, talking to her, even after she died. Said she thought maybe I felt like that, maybe I could use—

"Good God!" Franklin stopped short, pointed down the street. "What in the name of transportation is *that?*"

"It's your mother figure," Rosey said, smug, exultant. "Come to take you to school!"

Slowly, with enough backfiring to do a movie stunt driver proud, Willow Sloan rounded the corner and pulled into the Sanderses' driveway. Fastened less than securely to the top of her small white sedan, lurching from side to side with each turn, were two plastic balls shaped like giant scoops of chocolate ice cream. On top sat a Styrofoam mountain of whipped cream, and on top of that a huge cherry, its red enameled skin gleaming in the sun.

"You never saw the company car?" Rosey asked. "It's one of the major perks of Will's job. She told me it's embarrassing, but it beats walking."

"What the—?" He couldn't believe anything on four tires could look so ridiculous. "Why didn't you tell me?"

"I tried, big guy." Rosey sounded a lot more amused than seemed appropriate for someone whose boyfriend was about to be humiliated in front of an entire high school, grades nine through twelve. "I tried."

He watched, awestruck, horrified, as the top-heavy load shifted, then settled, and Willow brought the car to a stop.

Sundaes unlimited, it said in coffee-colored letters across the doors, too sweet to stop.

"Hi." Willow leaned out of the window. "Sorry I'm late. My dachshund threw up his breakfast."

"A likely story." Rosey grinned at Franklin, then at the slender girl behind the wheel. "Come on, Lin," she added, heading for the car. "I can't wait to see you drive up to school in this."

Franklin opened the passenger door, and Willow swept a pile of books and papers off the front seat. "This is some . . . er, car you've got," he told her, letting Rosey slip into the backseat before he climbed in front.

"No cool car jokes, please," Willow said. "No cornball fudgemobile cracks. I've heard 'em all."

"I bet you have." He liked the way she was dressed. Her navy fatigue seemed to have settled onto her khakis, no belt, no tucks, no fuss. Without the snappy, authoritative apron and cap, she hardly looked old enough to drive.

"Listen, it's pretty late." He sunk lower into his seat as they eased onto the highway. "I think I've already missed first period. Maybe we . . . I mean, I should probably just hoof it after all."

"No, you don't," Willow told him, slowing down. "I know that routine. After Tulip died, I found every reason in the world not to go to school. I took a semipermanent sabbatical!" Even on the straightaway she checked the side-view mirrors, as if she expected a chocolate avalanche at any minute. "I cut school for three months."

"Solid?"

"So solid I had to repeat my senior year."

"Wow. You've got me beat."

"I hope so, Mr. Tree." She turned, looked at him for such a long time he was afraid they'd swerve off the road. "I thought I was all alone. You're not."

Did Willow know about Rosey? He felt a strange relief until she added, "You can always talk to me, Mr. Tree."

He smiled awkwardly, said nothing.

"When somebody dies, everyone tells you to let it go."

How many times had he heard that? "Put it behind you." Wasn't that Stiller's favorite prescription?

"What they mean is stop *talking* about it. Stop reminding them." She forced a half-smile. "Shut up and sit down."

"She never told me." Rosey was studying Willow in the rearview mirror. "She never said a word."

Franklin knew how that worked. How after a while you stopped telling anyone, even your friends.

"But I would have understood," insisted Rosey. "That is, I think I would." Her voice dropped to a whisper. "Maybe I was too wrapped up in you and me. Too happy. Too . . . alive. . . ." She trailed off, was still.

They sat like that, the three of them, remembering. Even though he hadn't been able to convince Dud that Rosey had come back, Franklin was pretty sure Willow would believe him. All the people Dud loved were alive, but Willow had lost someone. She'd understand.

If they hadn't been seconds from school, if they hadn't been sitting in the lamest vehicle since Cinderella's pumpkin, he might have confided in his new friend. But instead Rosey broke the silence.

"Ask her how Fester's doing."

"How's Fester doing?" he repeated.

Willow turned, surprised. "How on earth did you know my dog's name?"

"Rosey told me."

"Oh. Right," she said, satisfied. "He liked Rosey a lot." They pulled into Archmont's parking lot. In seconds a small but animated crowd surrounded the sedan. Franklin was glad their windows were shut, glad he couldn't hear the remarks. "The dumb pooch is fine, I guess. I think it was his appetizer that upset his stomach."

"Appetizer?"

"Squirrel à la Fester."

"Sorry I asked." Rosey was laughing. "She looks great, doesn't she, Lin?"

Franklin supposed so, but suddenly he was more interested in someone he saw outside the car than anyone inside it. "Hey, Dud!" he called, opening the door. "Wait up!"

"Thanks for the ride," Rosey told Willow. "Mr. Manners thanks you too."

"Yo, Sanders!" someone called from the crowd. "What's that take? High-glucose?"

Franklin turned back. "Oh, yeah, Will. Thanks a lot."

"Nothing to it, Mr. Tree. Learn a ton." The laugh car edged cautiously toward the traffic, and Willow waved.

But Franklin was already headed toward school. "Did you see that?" He raced up the stairs, two at a time. "Rosey, come on. You're not going to believe this."

"Hey, Candy Man!" someone else yelled behind them. "Don't melt before homeroom!"

Rosey caught up with Franklin just as he caught up with Dud. And a girl. A girl they'd never seen before.

"Looks like Dud's found a friend." Rosey stared. "Of the female persuasion!"

She was tall, nearly as tall as Dud, and she was chattering away on fast-forward, her eyes Velcroed to his. The astonished pleasure on Dud's face was enough to make Franklin smile too. "I'll be damned," he said under his breath. "I'll be just plain damned."

"Sand Man." Dud greeted him with the hearty, hollow cheerfulness guys use when someone's watching. Someone they want to impress. "What's up?"

"Hey." Franklin grinned at Rosey, then at Dud, then at the strange girl. "Hey," he said again.

"Cheryl Ann, this is Lin." Dud was so proud, Franklin could feel his own heart contract. "Lin, this is Cheryl Ann. She's just moved to glamorous New Jersey from . . . where?"

"Charleston, South Carolina." She had an accent thick as cream and a constellation of freckles spread across her nose and cheeks. "So you're the famous athlete David's been boastin' about." She pronounced *athlete* as if it had three syllables, and she shook his hand like an adult.

"I play on the lacrosse team, that's all." Franklin put his arm around his lanky friend. Dud was the least athletic person on the planet, his arms and legs like distant, upstart kingdoms he couldn't control. But he loved sports, and he hadn't missed one of Franklin's games last spring. "The Dudster is a major fan." Pulling him closer. "Makes better calls than the refs."

Dud ducked away, self-conscious, grinning like a fine fool.

"Cheryl Ann and I are going to go take a dip into my Red Dwarf collection after school," he announced. "Want to join us?"

"Red Dwarf?" Rosey was clearly amazed. "She likes Red Dwarf?" She shook her head. "How did he find the only other person in the universe who likes that loser band?"

"Can't, Dud. Got an appointment with Dr. Doom." The last bell rang, and Franklin headed toward his locker, shrugging out of his backpack. He was pretty sure the invitation had been a matter of form, anyway. The last thing Dud needed was someone along on his first date.

"Wasn't it great? The look on his face just now?" Rosey sounded like somebody's mother, pleased and proud.

Franklin felt the same way. As if he'd handpicked Cheryl Ann, brought the two together. All day long, between classes, at lunch, during study hall, they caught glimpses of the new couple, glued to each other like kids used to be in junior high. After eighth period, the honeymoon was apparently still on; Franklin waved as Dud and Cheryl Ann drove off in Dud's Plymouth. Despite her new fuel pump, Loretta's engine sounded pingy, and Franklin was glad Dud lived only a few blocks away.

"I still can't believe it," Rosey said as they left school, headed downtown. "It's like all those corny movies—you know, where the class clown gets the prom queen?"

"I'll say." Franklin nodded at two men in work boots who passed them on the sidewalk. They were wearing the same bemused expression he'd seen on a dozen faces, the same look everyone who saw him talking to empty space wore. "I just hope a ride in that old heap of Dud's doesn't change her mind."

"Women don't care nearly as much about cars as men think they do." Rosey stopped, looked at the brick building across the street. "Is that Stiller's office?"

"How'd you know?"

"Lucky guess," she said, leading the way, then turning, grinning. "Plus, it looks like a prison."

August 25

It's my mother who tells me. She's waiting in the kitchen when I come home from the Tempo offices. I'm not planning to stay, just grab a sandwich, then head back to cover a town council meeting—business as usual. But right away I know something is wrong. Very wrong.

Mom would make a lousy poker player. Everything shows on her face. This time it is so crooked, so broken up, that I know someone's been hurt. I think it might be Dad, that he might have finally taken a half gainer off one of those dumb cliffs he loves to climb. A picture of him falling flashes through my mind just before she says, "Rose has had an accident." And for a minute it is still my father, not Rosey, dropping through space. Until Mom opens her arms. "I'm so sorry, honey. I'm so sorry." Until she holds me against her, and I realize it isn't Dad who's lost his balance, who is free-falling toward the ground. It's me.

Want to hear something unbelievable? The first thing I think when I hear about Rosey isn't, I hope she didn't suffer, or When can I see her? It's, Why couldn't it have happened after the lake? Like some angel of death was supposed to swoop down and check with me first: Okay, you decide, since you love her most. I can take her now, real quick. Or she can go slowly, lingering until after Labor Day, until after you two have had the best summer of your lives.

I know it sounds ridiculous, but I feel cheated. I didn't get to lie next to her at night on the dock, listening to the peepers start up all around the shore. I didn't get to lick the salt off that soft place at the back of her elbows. Or take her out in the boat when the water gets thick as Jell-O and the fish suck at the top of the water like they're trying to kiss the sky.

I'm finding out that's the way it is when someone dies, someone you love more than lacrosse or being right or even your mom. The minute you find out, it's not about them anymore. How could it be? They're gone, they're canceled. And they're never coming back. So now it's about you. Poor, lost, tragic, selfish-to-the-core you. It's about how much you miss them. How you can't touch or hear or look at anything without remembering. How you've actually soaked the whole front of your shirt crying. How much worse you feel than anyone anywhere has ever felt before. How different this makes you. Thunderstruck. Alone. Special.

And now I'm starting to think about the other stuff, too. Like whether she was hurting really bad, thrown on the side of the road, a wet rag doll in the rain. A beautiful rag doll in a stupid apron with a chocolate ice cream cone on the pocket. Or whether she said anything before she died. Whether it was something for me—a message. Maybe it would make me feel better about things, less guilty.

See, we had this fight just before she left for work this morning. A few weeks ago, when my cousin in Vermont got married, Rosey took time off to come to the wedding with me. She wore this pinkish-colored dress, and she looked so great it made me proud to be with her. But now she decides she can't turn right around and ask for more time off so we can leave for the lake three days early.

I tell her she's a big wimp, considering how they treat her like royalty at Sundaes Unlimited. I've seen the way Willow practically kisses her hand when she walks in, like she's afraid that any second Rosey will wake up and quit that lousy job.

"Look, Lin. I'm not going to go asking Will for special favors." I remember her, eyes small, foot on the running board of the Bubble Gum Machine. "She's got enough hassles with the creeps that don't even show up when they're supposed to."

"We're talking a few extra days here," I say. "It's not like you're asking for a raise." I make my voice harder, more sarcastic. "Which you deserve, by the way. And which they should have given you two weeks ago."

She jumps up into the seat and turns on the ignition. "I'm not going to sit here in the rain arguing with you." She shuts the door, snaps the window flaps. "Later, Lin."

Of course, people say stuff like that every day. Later, Lin. And they usually see you later. Later, Lin. Like we have plenty of time to fight and make up. I'm not going to sit here in the rain. . . . Like we have days and months and years.

Mrs. Mishimi has been crying. I can see the brown tracks in her makeup when she knocks on the door to my room. Mr. Mishimi is standing just behind her, his hand on her shoulder. "They gave us an envelope with some of her things in it," Mrs. Mishimi tells me. "We know she'd want you to have this." She hands me the bracelet, gold with Ichiban written on it in silver letters. Ichiban means "number one" in Japanese.

I look at the loop of gold in my hand. I gave it to Rosey last Christmas; she doesn't even take it off in the shower. And suddenly I feel her hand on my shoulder. I hear her voice. Lin-lin, knock it off. It's not as if I did this on purpose, you know. Please don't cry.

Sometimes I think I dreamed the whole thing—Mom in the kitchen with that twisted face, Mrs. Mishimi returning the bracelet. And the funeral. Did I dream them telling me about the funeral? Did I dream all three of them—Mom and Mr. and Mrs. Mishimi— standing outside my door, faces like shattered glass, saying Rosey would be buried day after tomorrow?

"I'm not going!" I yell. "I won't go!" Screaming like a bratty kid, slamming the door to keep out their broken, messy faces.

I'll never leave this room. I try to put Rosey's bracelet around my wrist, then throw it in the trash when it won't fit. I take the dumb blue dog off my radiator, the one Rosey won me at Slider Park amusements. One eye is missing, and the left ear is hanging by a thread. I lie down on my bed with the dog on my stomach, looking straight at me with its one black eye.

I'm not going to the funeral. In fact, I'm not getting out of bed. I'm staying here forever. Then it will be a dream, then Rosey will still be alive. She'll be right here next to me talking nonsense, wondering whether some fish want to be buried on land the way some people want to be buried at sea. Or she'll be cracking jokes about her venerable grandfather's venerable great-uncle with the single hair on his venerable chin.

Rosey in the Present Tense   99

If I don't get up, if I keep my eyes shut, she's standing next to the bed, hands on her hips, telling me she hasn't seen a messier room since she visited her aunt in California after an earthquake. Then she's clumping around in my sneaks, doing her Franklin Sanders impersonation. (She takes great big giant steps and puffs a lot. I don't think she looks much like me, but it always cracks me up.)

If I never leave this room, I'll never have to hear people talking about her in the past tense. Dear Rose, she was such a sweet girl, so young, so talented. I'll never have to listen to some pompous minister with his radio voice tell how happy she is now, safe from sorrow, ashes to ashes or whatever. If I don't move, if I just lie here, I can feel her fingers, light as air, smoothing back my hair, tickling my scalp. I can hear her say it again, just like she did that day at the falls. I think I love you.

And I don't need to say it back. Because she knows. She has to. Please, God, she has to know.

9

Dr. Stiller showed the faintest trace of emotion, a sliver of a frown that pulled the left side of his mouth down. It lasted only a second, his face righting itself before he handed the notebook back. "I see you decided not to take my suggestion," he said evenly. "You haven't rewritten any of these memories."

Franklin shifted his feet, careful to leave room for Rosey on the end of the couch. He grinned at his girl, who caught his smile and gave it back. How he had detested coming here until now. How he had loathed the cold vinyl of this black couch, the pale walls with their framed certificates and precisely placed African masks. But most of all he had hated the sound, the relentless, neutral droning, of Stiller's voice.

"I understand from your mother that you feel you've reached a plateau. She says you don't want to take your medication anymore."

Now that the shiny, crinkling couch held them both,

Franklin regarded it with something close to affection. He rubbed one hand over the place where it had been patched with black tape, then nodded. "Each new pill makes me sick in a whole new way." He didn't tell Stiller, and he hadn't told his mother, that he'd already stopped. That he'd needed to make sure Rosey wasn't some chemical hallucination, a Prozac dream.

"But she also tells me you feel as though Rosellen is still with you."

Franklin nodded again, studying the certificates, noticing for the first time that Stiller had studied in Italy and Greece.

Following his glance, Rosey laughed. "Doctor Doom sure put a lot of time and energy into learning to be a grouch, didn't he?"

Franklin's smile widened, and Stiller pounced. "I see that idea makes you happy." He leaned forward, tapping the notebook on Franklin's lap. "Is Rosellen with you in these memories? Is that it?"

Rosey's dark hair shone in the shaft of light that slipped through the half-shaded window. Her lips pursed, her brows arched. "Careful, Lin-san," she said. "He's trying to trap us."

"Yeah, I guess." Franklin knew she was right. He couldn't give the doctor too much.

Stiller took off his glasses now. "Do you think memories are enough?" He leaned back, slipping the glasses into his jacket pocket. "Memories fade, you know. How well do you remember your best friend from elementary school?"

"Move over." Rosey was wearing her give-'em-hell face. He shifted to the right side of the couch, and she lay down beside him, resting her head on his shoulder. "Two for the price of one," she said.

"Actually, I remember Terry Berlotti really well." Franklin breathed in the fresh baby scent of Rosey's neck, not daring to look at the watery, light-filled place where their bodies met. "He used to switch sandwiches with me when Mom made chipped beef. I really hate chipped beef."

"I see." But Stiller didn't look as if he saw anything. His eyes were shut, his fingers resting on his temples.

Rosey sat up, concentrating. "No good, Lin. He still thinks you're nuts."

"Would you say Rosellen is with you in any actual sense?" Stiller lifted his head, opened his eyes. "Do you and she have conversations?"

"See what I mean?" Rosey stood up and walked across the room. She ran her hand over the mahogany face of a mask on the wall above Stiller, sending a trickle of light into its cavernous grin. Then she leaned down, studied the pad on which the doctor had been writing since the session began. "Wish I could read his writing. It looks like a secret code or something."

"Shorthand," Franklin said before he could stop himself.

Stiller was interested again. His lifeless eyes showed a tiny spark. He rose from his chair, placed the pad on his desk. "You and Rosellen communicate in shorthand?"

How do I bail out of this one? Franklin felt like laughing, but he knew the feeling wouldn't last long. *I'll be coming here for the rest of my life once Mom hears about this.*

He waited for inspiration, his mind turning over and over

like a stalled engine. He grabbed a glass of water from the table beside the couch, drank the whole thing as slowly as he knew how, before he got an idea.

"I wrote a poem once," he said.

Stiller sat behind his desk now. "Yes, go on."

"I don't remember the words. But it was about dreams, how the difference between real life and dreams is like the difference between regular writing and shorthand."

"I see."

"That's how I communicate with Rosey." Franklin was proud of himself, high on his own ingenuity. "I dream about her."

"Oh." Stiller sounded slightly disappointed. "So you don't actually see her or talk to her?"

"Is your grandmother alive, sir?" Franklin was closing in for the kill.

"No," Stiller said. "She died when I was quite young."

"Do you see her or talk to her?"

"Certainly not."

Franklin smiled. "Then why would you think I can see or talk to Rosey?" He put the glass on the table beside the couch, folded his arms, making himself comfortable. "Get real, sir."

"You are totally, entirely sensational!" Rosey clapped her hands noiselessly. "A verbal acrobat. A wizard of words. A—"

"Well, I must say I'm relieved." Stiller glanced at the indecipherable symbols on his pad. "I think our, I mean your mother's, concerns were premature."

Franklin looked at Rosey, who was looking at Stiller. She was examining the doctor as if he were a banana or a grapefruit in the produce section, as if she were trying to decide whether he was ready yet. "I'm feeling much better, sir," he said. "I'm back in school." He crossed his arms noncommittally, stared at his own ankles, also crossed, at the foot of the couch. "Every day, I mean."

"In that case," Stiller said, "this may be a good time to— that is, I've told your mother I'd be referring your case."

He watched the doctor's expression change, all the authoritative folds collapsing into softness and panic. *God*, he thought, *this man really likes my mother*.

He uncrossed his arms, stared at his therapist. He tried to picture Dr. Stiller, his angular, small-eyed face next to his mother's. *He can't even mention her without turning purple!*

"I understand that your mother has mentioned to you that—I believe you know we're personal friends?"

Determined not to make things easy, Franklin barely nodded.

"Because I'm no longer, strictly speaking, that is, objective. . . ." Stiller stood again, his pad pinned to his chest like a shield. "And because you appear to be out of the woods, therapeutically, you know, I've decided to recommend you see another counselor." He smiled his sliver smile. "Mrs. Wollenski is a grief specialist. I think you'll find her helpful."

Suddenly Franklin saw the light. "You're dumping me?" He tried not to sound too eager, too hopeful.

"I'm not sure 'dumping' is the right word." Dr. Stiller's smile turned to a frown.

"Yes, it is," Rosey said. "Dumping is exactly what he's doing, Lin. Isn't it great?"

"It sure is!" Franklin spoke without thinking.

"No, son," Stiller assured him. "I'm simply reassigning your case." Another watery smile. "For your best interest."

Franklin settled back against the squeaky leather, beaming at Rosey. "Yes, sir," he agreed. *No more prescriptions. No more hours in this stale, bleached room. No more listening to Stiller's endless talkathons!* "Okay, sir."

Then they were standing, shaking hands, and Franklin was listening to the man's unctuous prognosis. Stiller was sure his patient would heal, certain he'd overcome his "fixation."

Franklin nodded, smiling, holding the pose until he could make his break. Until he could leave that stifling office, could pass the reception desk without making another appointment, could walk down the stairs and away from that building for the last time, Rosey at his side.

But the following week, when Stiller came to the house, an awkward, civilian smile on his long face, when the two of them sat facing each other across the coffee table, Franklin decided seeing the doctor at the office hadn't been so bad after all. "Mom'll be right down," he said, sounding like the teenage son in a fifties TV show. "Mom!" He yelled it into the air behind them, feeling the minutes drag. Suddenly, he sprang to his feet. "I'll go tell her you're here."

"Linny, you're taking this much too hard." Rosey followed him up the stairs, stood beside him while he knocked on his mother's bedroom door.

"Easy for you to say," Franklin whispered. "Your mother's married to someone you like."

His mother opened the door, the scent of gardenias and honey exploding into the narrow hall.

"Your date's here." Franklin bit the word off short, as if he didn't like its taste. "The King of Hearts, the Prince of Moves, the—"

"It's not as if she's going to marry him, you know." Rosey wasn't taking this nearly seriously enough. Her small shoulders were pulled up like a fullback's, her whole body fighting laughter.

"Honey, I wish you'd be a little more understanding," Helen Sanders said, slipping past Franklin, all rustling taffeta and knockout smells. "It's not as if we're getting married, you know."

He tried to dislodge the pictures forming inside his head. Stiller across the breakfast table. Stiller stroking Mingo while he watched TV. Or maybe there wouldn't even be a TV anymore, maybe they'd all just sit around and listen to the doctor lecture!

Downstairs in the living room they stood for interminable minutes, talking nonsense. Franklin was rigid with discomfort, but Rosey was definitely enjoying herself. "Aren't you going to make tea?" she asked. "The good doctor looks like he could use a crumpet."

"So where are you kids off to?" Franklin tried to keep it light, moving them toward the door as he spoke. "Mom, I'll expect you back at a reasonable hour. Don't make me call the party."

"Or cucumber sandwiches," suggested Rosey. "I could whip some up in a sec." Franklin hadn't seen her so silly, so high since . . . since . . .

Rosey in the Present Tense   107

"Very funny, son of mine," his mother said. "Very funny." She didn't seem to mind his clowning around. She looked, to his horror, as though nothing much at all could bother her—a serene, unflappable float in her walk and voice. "What are you up to while we're out gallivanting?" (A quick flash of a smile at Stiller.)

Franklin didn't want to consider what "gallivanting" might encompass. "Dud and his new woman are coming over, that's all."

Before Stiller, his mother would have drawn things out, found any feeble excuse to stay, to meet someone so important to Dud. Not now, though. Now she sighed, shrugged. "Maybe I'll get to meet this mystery woman next time." She stepped back as the doctor opened the door, crinkled past him, smiling again.

Franklin watched the therapist, noticed him look at his mother with a sort of greedy approval, as if the red dress, her new shoes, were offerings, glittering tributes to the Great God Stiller.

"I never liked him," he told Rosey as soon as the door was closed, "but now I *hate* him."

"I sink zee patient has made incredible progress." Rosey's shrink accent was a mixed bag, a mad scientist and an absent-minded professor. "He iz experiencing zee full range of his emotions. Und best of all, he iz jealous of his muzzer's boy-friend. Oedipus! Oedipus!" She grinned wickedly, walked toward him, swiveling her hips in a triumphant, sexy slink. "Vee knew you had it in you!"

He couldn't help smiling. Couldn't help loving her. "You," he said, pointing, laughing, "I could stand to see on a regular basis. Where's the couch? I think we should get started right away."

"Hey." Dud had opened the front door, was walking, shedding his jacket as he went, into the living room. Thornton galloped past him, stopped short in front of Rosey, growling. Still outside the door, Cheryl Ann was waiting to be asked in. "I knocked," Franklin's friend told him, "but you were . . . busy."

It was obvious Dud had overheard the conversation with Rosey; he was wearing the look that said, Why can't you get better? Why can't things be normal again? "Okay if Cher and I come in?"

Franklin watched Mingo arch his back, then run a crazy end pattern toward the basement door. Rosey leaned down to ruffle the fur behind Thornton's collar, breaking the light there, bending it like reflections on moving water. "Sure," he said. "We . . . I rented this great video." He wondered if the spaniel felt anything as Rosey stroked him. Raindrops, maybe? A rush of warmth? "It's a seventies horror flick, with giant killer termites and some guy who eats steroids for breakfast."

"You mean like me, my man?" Dud puffed up his nonexistent biceps, and Cheryl Ann, who joined them now, pretended to be impressed.

"My goodness, David," she said, putting her hand on his arm, rolling her pale eyes, "you just better stop that working out, you hear?" She giggled as the two of them nestled into the couch in front of the TV. "Else they'll be sending you off to the 'Lympics. Pretty soon you'll be too famous to 'sociate with the likes of us."

"Aren't they great together?" Rosey was genuinely delighted. Curled beside the strangely docile Thornton on the floor, she watched the new couple. "Dud still looks like he can't believe it."

"No, no. I'll never forget you little people," Dud promised. "I'll send Christmas cards every year. Hand-signed, too." He grinned magnanimously. "No autograph stamps for me."

More giggles from Cheryl Ann. Everything Dud said seemed to amuse her. Which was only fair, Franklin decided, since everything she did obviously sent Dud into orbit. It was like watching the happiest, soupiest chick flick imaginable, seeing the way the two of them touched whenever they could, the way they smiled continually, hugely. Borderline pathetic.

"So how'd you get two names?" Franklin asked, forcing himself into Cheryl Ann's line of vision.

Dud's girl brought herself out of the unnatural twist that had swiveled her whole torso toward Dud. "Fate," she said. "I was born in the South. Everyone down there has two names." She laughed. "You know. Billy Bob. Deborah May. That sort of thing.

"My mom says I'll have to change it for concerts. She says no one will take me seriously if I don't."

"Concerts?"

Cheryl Ann shrugged and smiled at Dud now, fell back against him. "My mom's got this dream I'm goin' to go and be a classical pianist. As crazy as she is about Chopin and Schumann, it would tickle her jus' to death, seein' me on stage."

"As in famous?"

"Well, probably not," Cheryl Ann said. "But I've been takin' lessons for simply forever."

"Don't let the gorgeous exterior fool you," Dud said. "This woman is talented. Juilliard talented."

"No kidding?" Franklin was as astonished as he sounded. "That's great." You never knew people, he thought. You never knew what surprises they had packed away inside the folds of their brains, hidden in their hearts.

"David, will you stop braggin' on me?" Giggles. Touching. Smiles.

"Who would figure," Rosey said, reading Franklin's mind again, "there were sonatas behind that southern drawl? Or a passion for Red Dwarf!"

They settled into the movie, everyone except Franklin. Each time he looked up to catch Rosey's eye, to see if she thought a scene was as outrageous as he did, he was faced with something even more preposterous: budding romance. Dud and Cheryl Ann held each other tight during every grisly bloodbath, cuddled during the brief dialogue bits that separated murders. As he tried not to watch them, Franklin was surprised again—this time by himself.

It made him uneasy, their handholding, their touching. No, it was more than uneasy. It made him remember what he and Rosey couldn't have anymore. It made him want to avert his eyes, glue himself to the screen. It made him skittish, embarrassed, tense. It made him—the feeling was new, but he knew its name after all—jealous.

How could I? he asked himself. *How could I be jealous of my best friend? He's always been the third wheel, always on the outside looking in.* Sure, Dud had hung out with all the kids. He'd been their official clown, their designated driver, the boy who was every girl's confidant, nobody's crush. *But now, he's got a chance to find out what it's like when the jokes are over. When someone takes you seriously.*

The excitement, the rush, of first love came back to Franklin. Like a ghost of itself, like the sound of laughter that reaches you from an open car and then fades. *I know Dud deserves this. Why can't I be happy for him?*

"Because we deserved it, too." Rosey answered his thought. She came and sat on the arm of the small, stuffed chair Franklin had chosen rather than share the couch with Dud and Cheryl Ann. "We didn't do anything wrong, Lin-lin. We deserved the same chance, didn't we?"

Her silliness, her light mood, were gone. Franklin saw her eyes fill, soft pools spilling over. He saw their rims glisten as if her tears were real, as if he could reach over and touch them, moisten his finger, his cheek. "It was just a few seconds, Lin. A few lousy seconds." She shook her head. "If only I'd worn my dumb seat belt," she said. "If only I'd seen that stupid truck."

10

When he woke the next morning, Franklin thought maybe he was still dreaming. Rosey wasn't wearing jeans or her T-shirt from California. She had a kimono on, and her hair was pulled back with a comb. The kimono was dark blue, almost navy, with white birds flying across it, their long legs dangling like ribbons from under their wings.

"Hi, you," she said, kneeling beside his bed. "I thought you'd never wake up."

She'd always been pretty, but now she looked more beautiful than anyone Franklin had ever seen. In fact, she made *beautiful* another useless word, one that couldn't possibly measure up. Her skin was glowing, rich as cream, and her eyes were deeper than he remembered. When she bent close to him, they had a distant shine, like coins sparkling at the bottom of a well.

"Guess what, Lin-san?" Her voice was excited—a little

girl's. "I found out who's been waiting for me. I found out who was behind the screen."

He loved the animation, the liveliness in her face and tone. But something set off alarms inside him, something that threatened the time they'd had, the truce with death and grief.

"It was Baba!" She pushed herself up, perched beside him on the quilt. "Only not like she was when we saw her, you know?" She bent her knees under the kimono, wrapped her arms around her ankles, and he smiled when he saw she was still wearing jeans and sneakers under the exotic robe. "She was here while you were sleeping."

"Here?" Franklin knew he was awake now, knew something was wrong.

"She looked so lovely." Rosey's color, her joy were all new. "She wasn't an *o-ba-san*, an old one. She was a young girl, my age. She wore a beautiful dress, like a geisha in a teahouse. And she had this one for me, said we'd be like sisters." She glanced at one of her liquid sleeves. "Her face was bright as a moon, Lin. Or a lantern."

"Wait," he said. "How could Baba get here? She's too sick."

"She wasn't sick at all. And she was right here. I saw her." She stood up, walked toward the window, her profile shimmering in the early light. "She asked me to say that poem for her, you know, about the bridge?" She turned from the dawn and faced him, grinning. "I said it right this time, all the way through."

"No chopsticks?"

"No chopsticks." Her smile was tender, hesitant now. "Baba said she'd help me. Show me the way back."

"Back?" *No. No. No.*

"I don't belong here, Lin. You know I don't." Before he could answer, tell her yes, she did, she belonged with him and he belonged with her, his mother knocked on the door.

"You awake?" she asked, opening the door, surprised to see he was. "Listen, honey, the Mishimis just called." She looked tousled, as if the call might have caught her in bed. She'd been sleeping late on weekends to make up for all those 5 A.M. film shoots. Her voice was foggy, apologetic. "Sad news."

He knew before she told him. Rosey's grandmother had died in her sleep last night. "I guess it's a blessing," Helen Sanders said, tightening the sash of her robe, watching him with careful, worried eyes. "Harold says she hasn't been herself ever since . . ." More worry, more apology. "Well, you know."

"I know, Mom," Franklin told her. "It's okay." As if he'd just given her permission, his mother finally sat beside him on the bed. They stayed like that, not talking, not needing to.

The morning of Baba's funeral, there was another call from Willow. "Hey, Mr. Tree," she said. "Guess what?"

"What?"

"I'm going to go hear a real live poet laureate read today. Wanna come?"

"I can't." Franklin, whose mother was giving what she called a "dog-and-pony show" for a client in Chicago, wasn't going to the chapel with him. He'd have to get there on his own, and he'd have to get there quickly. "Sorry."

"It's Rita Dove," Willow said, as if the name might change his mind. "Rosey used to tell me what a great poet you are. I just thought, you know, it takes one to know one."

"Listen," Franklin said. "I'd really like to. Any other time. Okay?" She sounded so happy, so up, he couldn't tell her about the funeral. Not now. "I gotta go." He noticed his feet, saw he'd forgotten to change into dress shoes.

"Sure." She didn't sound hurt, just surprised. "Our whole MAT class—sorry, Modern American Thought—is going. We got the first five rows. You positive?"

"Yeah. 'Bye." He raced upstairs, grabbed his best shoes out of the closet, then tore back down again. Rosey was standing at the end of the driveway when he opened the front door and hopped, one foot in a shoe, the other still in a sock, after her.

"Hey," he said, studying her as they waited for the bus. "How come no beautiful dress? I thought Baba liked you in a kimono?"

"She does."

Present tense, Franklin thought. *I'm not the only one who can't let go.*

"But it's such a pain to pick up the hem every time I walk." Rosey climbed onboard when the bus pulled up, found a seat toward the back. "Guess I'm just not the swishy type."

He looked approvingly at her graceful arms, the soft roundness under her T-shirt. "You're my type, swishy or not," he told her.

For a minute Rosey was preoccupied, silent. He assumed she was thinking about Baba, but then she turned to him, smiling, proud, as if she'd just worked something out. "I like her, Lin," she said. "I hadn't thought of Will, but she's perfect."

"Perfect?" Franklin felt about two years old when she smiled at him like that—matter-of-fact, grown-up, galaxies away. "What are you talking about?"

"About when I'm gone." Rosey put her hand up to keep him from interrupting. "Seeing as how you never took that vow of chastity, you're going to need a girlfriend—"

"Hold the phone, Mishimi," he warned. "Stop right there."

"Will goes to State, Lin. And if you're there too—"

"A," announced Franklin, doing one of his lists, "I bombed so badly on the SATs, I'm lucky if they let me out of high school; B, I don't date older women; and C, you are altogether nuts if you think for one second I'm in the market for—"

"Chill, Linny." They'd reached their stop, and he followed her as the bus door whooshed open. "I just mean, love comes in different sizes, you know?"

He didn't feel like an argument, didn't have any desire to speculate about the future. It was a relief, then, to see the Mishimis waiting at the door of the funeral parlor, to catch up to them, waving, and rush inside.

Baba's funeral wasn't at all like Rosey's. For one thing, there were very few people. For another, there wasn't much crying. The service seemed slow and still. Franklin found himself looking over the heads in front of him, out the windows, to where spring was only a few weeks away.

"Baba loved being outside," Rosey told him, following his glance. "She grew up near Lake Biwa, and she used to fill her house with plum blossoms and willow branches."

He thought of Rose's grandmother, her brave English, her fearless heart. He tried to imagine Baba young, with long dark hair and a waist as slim as Rosey's. He tried to picture her shy, in love.

"She and my grandfather were married in a Shinto ceremony. He died before I was born, but she talked to him all the time. She used to have a Buddhist priest come to our house and offer prayers for him."

Franklin leaned toward her, whispered. "I thought she went to church with you and your parents?"

"She did." Rosey nodded. "Every Sunday, like clockwork. She said since her parents believed one thing, her children another, she had no intention of betting her soul on who was right and who was wrong."

Franklin smiled, hoping it was just the light in the dim chapel that made Rosey seem fainter, less *there*, than she had in a long time. He sat with her, holding Baba in his mind, letting the service filter in and out of his attention. Slow music, slower talk, and a cluster of bright, scentless flowers at the front of the room. He glanced at the families around him, wished that his mother had been able to come.

But it was just the two of them, Rosey and Franklin, who walked with the Mishimis back into the clean morning light, into the world where other people, who hadn't been touched by death today, were eating pancakes or buying carpet or changing their oil. And it was only Franklin whom Rosey's parents thanked for coming, whom they invited, as they had before, to visit anytime he wanted.

He hugged her mother, shook her father's hand, then struck off across town, in a direction opposite from home. Without discussion, as if they'd agreed ahead of time, he and Rosey headed for the woods outside the county park. Silent, they walked past the last intersection, then along the bike path and into the shade. The hum of traffic faded, the industrious rattle of a woodpecker followed them, and sometimes a dead tree limb sighed in the wind overhead. They scuffed their way through last year's leaves and brown vines that would soon glisten with three-fingered mittens of poison ivy. They clambered over mossy logs and piles of limestone, winding along the trench an ancient river had dug in the forest floor. Until they heard the familiar chatter, rounded a bend, and came to the waterfall.

Rosey stood still, then sighed a tiny sigh, like a baby in its sleep. "Remember what I told you here?"

Remember? How many times had he tormented himself for not saying it back right away? *I love you, Rosey Mishimi. I love you too*.

"I feel just the same right now," she said.

"But you're going, aren't you?" He didn't really need to ask. He smelled the charged, damp air coming from the falls; felt the slant of the pebbly ground underfoot. But nothing around them seemed real.

She nodded. "I have to." She turned toward the water coursing over the stones, the halo of light that hummed just above it. "I wish I could explain. I'm so tired, Linny. If we could have what we used to . . ."

Was it a real tear he saw, gathering into fullness at the rim of her eye, then slipping toward the corner of her mouth? Like a river going home, he thought. Was that how she felt?

The light around her throbbed, shivered. "The love is still there. It's just . . . the need, the hungry feeling, is gone." She faced him, and for the first time he saw how exhausted she looked. A sprinter in her last lap. "It's almost as if I love you more, with that out of the way. Do you understand? A little?"

He nodded, but he didn't. Couldn't.

"Don't be afraid. It's sweet afterward, Lin. That's a promise."

He swallowed, turned away. He watched the water, a glistening wall that seemed to race ahead and stay still all at the same time. He thought of sitting in church when he was little. *In my Father's house are many mansions.*

"I came back so you'd know. So we could say good-bye."

He remembered who he'd been after Rosey died, the kid who couldn't get out of bed, who had trouble deciding which socks to wear, whose days pressed down on him like the low ceiling of a small, cruel house.

Then he thought about the others, the ones who never got to say good-bye: parents, children, friends whose lives were changed in a second, whose love was extinguished in the time it takes to set a bomb or crash a plane or shoot a revolver. He knew he should feel lucky, he knew he should count himself blessed. And he knew he should do what Rosey was waiting for him to do. He should let her go.

"Baba says there's only time between us, Lin." She touched the back of his neck, kissed his cheek. Her lips brushed his skin with a warmth so slight it might have come from a cloud unveiling the sun. "It will pass, you know."

He wanted to be selfless, noble, but he felt petulant as a spoiled child. "Time can take forever."

"Or it can go so quickly, you wish you could stop it." She smiled, a tight grown-up smile. "I blinked and I was dead, Lin. I blinked, and I was here again."

"It feels like I'll never stop loving you." Tears were working their slow, salty way down his cheeks, into his mouth. "Like I'll always need you."

That sad smile again, that look that sent her spinning away from him. "You're seventeen. You'd make a lousy monk."

He remembered wanting to stay a virgin forever. "I've considered it," he told her.

"Each time you love someone, I'll be there." The sun had gotten higher, brighter, and Rosey was fading into it, white on white. "Not looking over your shoulder, not getting in the way." She tried to take his hands, her fingers slipping, spilling off his. "Here." She reached out, touched his chest, her hand splintering, shedding fireworks of light.

He found her dark eyes in the pool of light. "Can't you wait a bit, Rosey? You know, give me some time to get used to the idea?"

He was bargaining, shaking. "I mean, Baba knows where you belong." *Selfish, selfish, selfish.* "But what about me? Where do I fit in? How am I supposed to go on living without you?"

She leaned close, the tips of her hair fiery with sunlight. "You'll have friends, Lin. You'll fall in love. You'll write a book . . ."

He couldn't afford to feel her confusion, see her pain. A rush of blood stiffened all the muscles in his face. "Oh, I get it now." His smile was sarcastic, his nods huge, exaggerated. "It all makes sense. Deathless prose. *That* will fix everything!"

"Listen, Lin." She backed away from him, held up her hands. As if he could touch her. "Baba says you'll understand, you'll change, you'll grow."

"I don't want to change, damn it!" He sounded desperate, infantile, even to himself. "I don't want to grow." But underneath the yelling, behind the hurt, was the fear. *Rose, I can't. I can't do this.*

The light around her grew agitated, full of motes and swirling. "Oh, Linny. Don't cry, please don't cry."

He stopped short, as if she'd barked a command instead of begun crying herself. He blinked into the fierce light. And he saw her, really saw her.

She was dissolving, slipping away. Her outlines were already lost to the white-hot light. But what remained, what shivered and stammered in front of him, was her face, streaming with tears. Yearning was there, and love and loss—a loss that was even bigger than his. And how he hated the knowledge, the certainty, that only he could give her what she longed for.

"Rose." The name sounded like a wrong note; it hurt his mind to hear it. "I want you to be where you need to be." He searched those bright, torn eyes, concentrated on the memory of her hands in his. "If you're not hungry for me, if it's something else you need, I want you to be full." He fought to keep his voice firm, even. "I want you to be happy." It was important, this time, to tell her. Not to let the words go unsaid. "I love you, Rosey." He paused, full of memories, out of time. "I love you, and I want you to go."

He didn't feel noble or frightened or even romantic. He was part of a whole, running on instinct, doing what he had to. Which was to watch Rosey's face get swallowed by the light. A minute ago, he might have screamed out, might have run after her. But not now. Frozen, he saw her eyes, like dark seeds being buried, disappear into the glow.

"Look. Look." Her skin, her mouth, the hands he couldn't hold—everything blazed, then vanished. Only her voice was left, full of wonder. "Baba's here, Lin. Do you see her?"

He stared into the miniature sunset where she'd stood. He saw nothing, not even a shadow. "Oh, Rose," he whispered, tearless. "It's not so hard. I want you to know, it doesn't hurt so much."

"Less and less, Lin. That's a promise, too."

"Less and less," he repeated, to make himself believe it. His left hand, as if it had a mind or a heart all its own, reached toward her voice, but the light peeled away in front of him, shimmering like fog in a headlight. "Did I mention that I love you?"

"You did." Disembodied, distant, her voice had stopped shaking. "Don't cry."

"Who's crying?" He couldn't see. Water. Light. Tiny crystal droplets, reflecting everything, nothing.

"Oh, Lin." Her voice was farther away still, an echo from a place he could no longer find. "Lin-lin, you should see—"

"Mishimi!" He closed his eyes against the light, covered them with his hands. Even so, he could feel the burning, the white heat. "Mishimi!"

"You should see."

But Franklin knew there was nothing to see. Slowly, he opened his eyes, then lowered his hands, still cupped as if he held something precious. The light was gone. The water gurgled and spattered. A twig snapped under his weight. A brown bird—he couldn't tell what kind—fluttered out of the woods behind him and threw itself, calling loudly, into the sky.

August 25

It's weird. I've got only a few pages left in this notebook, and I've been wondering how to finish it. Then I had this dream about Rosey last night. Weird again, because it's exactly a year since she died.

My Rosey dream wasn't in color, no special effects, not even a plot. It was more like a conversation that got interrupted when I woke up. I don't remember much of what we said to each other. (I think I told her that Charlie Strand never graduated, and I think she said she liked my haircut.) But it left me with a quiet, sleepy peace inside. As if she'd been checking up on me, and everything was fine.

That's more or less the way I've felt the last couple of months. It's partly because of the counselor Stiller sicced on me. Turns out she's a lot better at listening than he was. And a lot less pill-happy. We start each session by talking about Rosey or anything else I want. Then she asks about school, lacrosse, stuff like that. She says

I'm doing great, that once classes begin I'll be too busy, and too uncrazy, to keep seeing her.

I'm starting at State right after Labor Day, but I've already put in a lot of time on campus. Will has dragged me to a ton of lectures and two pretty good concerts there. She even had me sit in on one of her lit classes. Everybody around here rags on State, but I'll tell you, that class was rough. I mean, I'm going to have to do some serious reading. Thinking, too.

Dud's already left for school; he flew out west last week. (His dad has been teaching him Kansas football cheers since he was old enough to talk, so there was never much doubt where he'd be going to college.) He won't be home for Thanksgiving, but Cheryl Ann has a holiday recital at Juilliard, so he's looking forward to Christmas already. He called yesterday and said he met three girls at freshman orientation but he still prefers mint juleps to cornfields, something like that.

I asked Mom if we could keep Thornton while Dud's away, but she said Mingo would have a heart attack, and I guess she's right. Anyway, I promised I'd go over to the Duddens' on weekends and run around with Thornton and that drooly chew toy of his. It's shaped like a newspaper, but it's made of rubber and it squeaks. Thornton loves the thing, and I know how to throw it with just the right twist so he has to double back to get it.

Stuff at home is pretty normal again, especially Mom. She's a lot more relaxed, and best of all, she's dating a new guy. His name is Gerald. He sweats a lot and tells really lame jokes, but she seems to like him. And anybody's better than Stiller the Stiff. For a while there, I thought we were going to be one big happy family therapy session. I mean, Mom was talking about "personal boundaries" and "stress factors." Pretty scary!

Another close call: My SATs weren't as bad as I thought. I placed out of freshman comp, so I'm going to be in this special English class, where I'll get to write poetry and maybe even plays. Will's taking it, too, because it's a level 3 course and she's a junior. I showed her one of my poems, and she said it reminded her of Walt Whitman. I wish! Still, I love it when she says things like that—wild, Will thinks about how her family's going to come back as a forest in their next lives, how Sundaes puts urethane in their syrup to make it shine, and how I'm almost the greatest poet who ever lived.

Before you go getting any ideas, Will is not my girlfriend or anything. She's just a girl who's a friend. I still miss my Rose like crazy. But it's like she said at the waterfall: There's only time between us. At first, that didn't seem like much to hang on to. But there are moments, gut flashes, when I think I understand. Like when I catch a Jackie Wilson song on an oldies station ("Lonely Tear Drops" always tore Rosey up) or see the way those lemon-colored flowers in her garden at school have opened.

See, time doesn't have to be set up in neat little packages, past, present, future. That's how we think about it, but if you stop and feel stuff, you know it's really all blended together—what you did as a kid, the things you remember from yesterday, who you'll be tomorrow. You can't have one without the others. And you certainly can't lose someone you love and go on living the same life you did before you met them.

So now it's as if Rosey's behind that screen she talked about. I can't reach out and hold her, can't even look at her, but I know she's with me. Seeing isn't always believing. Sometimes it's the last thing you need.

There are bad days, of course. Days I fight to keep from remembering that no matter what I do or say or think, she's never going to take my hand again, never going to look at me cross-eyed in the middle of a kiss or point across the room to absolutely nothing while she swipes the olives off my pizza. Still, most of the time I look at what I've felt and been through, and it's strange, but I wouldn't want to go back to being that jerk who took it all for granted. I mean, when I was with Rosey every day, when I could see her anytime I wanted, I didn't love her the way I do now. I didn't see how precious every second is, how each moment makes a difference. I wish I had, but I didn't. Maybe most people don't.

I wrote a poem for Rosey this morning, and I took it to the cemetery. It's the kind of place that doesn't allow big monuments, so you have to look for the grave by number. You check the signs like you're in a hotel lobby: Plots 346–589. Then you walk down the row till you come to Rosey's stone.

And Baba's. According to the Mishimis, they were all set to send Baba's ashes to Japan, where Rosey's grandfather is buried, when they found a second will. Baba apparently decided that Rosey needed her more than her husband, who'd done fine sleeping by himself for over twenty years. So that's how it ended up—Rosey and her grandmother, side by side.

Both markers are set flat in the grass with white mums around them. (Mrs. Mishimi wanted roses, but the cemetery has some rule about plants not being too tall.) Rosey's stone is pink marble with swirls of purple in it, but there's no fancy inscription. It's like the plaque in the garden at Archmont; it just lists the year she was born, the year she died, and her name.

I guess I wanted to make it up to her for not saying the words when she was alive, for not even being able to write them when she died. So today, I sat down as close to the stone as I could without crushing the mums, and read the poem out loud. There was a man in shirtsleeves repairing a fence on the other side of the cemetery and a family at a plot a few yards away. They probably thought I was nuts, but who cares?

You were, I am, we'll be,
There's only time between us—
but, Rosey-san, it seems so long.
For months, I found your face,
your scratchy laugh in crowds,
watched you move like water
through the dark of every dream.

You told me I would grow,
you said I'd start to change—
Ichiban, that's just half true.
'Cause if the scent of roses
comes softly after rain,
or someone sings off-key,
I still turn and look for you.

It doesn't always rhyme, but none of my poems do. Will says that's okay; she says the really good ones don't. I don't know if this is a really good one, but I think Rosey would have liked it. I'm going to write some more, maybe enough for a whole book. I think she'd like that, too.